Jake and
Thanks for
Literacy is lit! (I'm a corny
English teacher, sorry.) I hope you
enjoy and share with friends!

The Emaciated Man and Other Terrifying Tales from Poe Middle School

by Evan Baughfman

M000045084

No part of this work may be reproduced or transmitted in any form or by any means, electronic or mechanical, including photocopying and recording, or by any information storage or retrieval system without the proper written permission of the copyright owner unless such copying is expressly permitted by federal copyright law. Thurston Howl Publications is authorized to grant permission for further uses of the work in this book. Permission must be obtained from author or the publication house. Address requests for permission to make copies of material to the email address jonathan.thurstonhowlpub@gmail.com.

THE EMACIATED MAN AND OTHER TERRIFYING TALES FROM POE MIDDLE SCHOOL

Copyright © 2020 by Evan Baughfman

Edited by Thurston Howl

First Edition, 2020. All rights reserved.

A Thurston Howl Publications Book
Published by Thurston Howl Publications
Lansing, Michigan

jonathan.thurstonhowlpub@gmail.com

Printed in the United States of America

*For Ashley, for everything,
including giving me time to write,
even when I may have been wrong*

Table of Contents

WELCOME TO POE

WELCOME TO EDGAR ALLAN Poe Middle School, where the coursework's not as frightening as what stares and whispers at you from the dark.

The school is built over a Civil War battlefield, which could explain why a phantom chill and a vaguely rotten smell permeate throughout many of its classrooms and hallways.

It could also explain why misfortune befalls so many of Poe's students today.

Has the blood spilled in the past forever cursed the land? Did that carnage draw in sinister forces that still require a constant offering of screams and pain?

Whatever the case may be, the young people of Poe Middle do their best to navigate the perils of adolescence while simultaneously surviving the horrors of things lurking in the shadows.

Named after a successful author of the mysterious and macabre, Poe Middle School has many of its own stories to share. And not all of them have happy endings.

Middle school is a scary place, after all. And, at Poe, that is especially true.

It takes a courageous soul to enter these school grounds.

You have what it takes, though.

Right?

Sure, you do.

Come on in, then, if you dare.

Listen closely to what's told to you.

It just might save you from whatever welcomes you in the dark . . .

LOUD MOUTHS

INSIDE THE EDGAR ALLAN Poe Middle School library, Gilbert stood before a towering bookshelf and groaned. "Man," he said, "who would want to read any of these stupid books?"

A girl he recognized from P.E. class stood a few feet away. "Hey," he said in a loud whisper. "Hey, you. Girl!"

She thumbed through a collection of poetry and completely ignored him. But when did that ever stop Gilbert?

"Hey, girl," he said louder. "Hello? Helloooooo, I'm talking to you. The longer you ignore me, the more annoying I get."

The girl turned, glaring at him. "What?"

"That's right, listen to me," Gilbert said, smiling. "Some of these books have got like a million pages. Do you think we'd get knocked out if a couple of them fell off the shelf and hit us in the head?"

"What are you talking about?"

"They're like bricks. Our skulls could totally cave in if these things hit us at the right angle!"

"Sure... Whatever." The girl stalked off with a book of poems.

"Hey, come on!" Gilbert shouted after her, grinning. "Where

are you go—?"

"Shhh!" the librarian scolded from behind the checkout desk. She held a taut index finger in front of her lips.

Gilbert couldn't believe he was actually wasting lunchtime in the library. It proved how badly he wanted answers, how badly he needed a solution to his problem. He was desperate for anything that would help keep him quiet.

He was a talker. No matter how many times his teachers called home, no matter how many times his mom took away his television, skateboard, and video games, his brain always came up with things for his lips to say. It wasn't his fault. He was just made this way.

Gilbert had heard rumors of a special book hidden among the plethora of titles in the library, a magical book of spells that supposedly solved students' troubles.

Apparently, his cousin, Evelyn, had used the book to get rid of her acne. Her face once looked like a minefield. Now, though, she modeled in ads for one of the stores at the mall.

Gilbert had laughed when Evelyn first told him her story. She had to be making it all up. But then she showed him a pair of selfies on her phone. The first one featured her sullen face covered in red-hot pimples. The next photo, dated a day later, showed Evelyn beaming because her skin had smoothed out and no longer displayed a single blemish.

"No filter," Evelyn had said.

"No way!" Gilbert had declared.

He knew, however, that Evelyn was telling the truth. She'd never lied to him before.

Gilbert had to get his hands on that book.

He needed a similarly speedy turnaround for his issue.

A voice whispered behind Gilbert. "Can I help you?"

He turned to find the librarian standing there. She wore all black. A raven pendant dangled from a necklace around her throat, and her hair was dyed the color of night. "Is there something in particular you are looking for? And, please, whisper."

Gilbert said in his quiet voice, "I want that secret book of spells everyone talks about."

"Secret book of spells?" The librarian looked puzzled. "There is no secret book of spells here."

"Oh," said Gilbert, defeated.

"There is only *this* book of spells."

The librarian grabbed a thin, gray book from directly in front of Gilbert. There was no title or numbered label on its spine or cover.

The woman handed the book over to Gilbert. "Be careful with this. It's very delicate."

The book was rough to Gilbert's touch. "It feels weird."

"It's made of dragon skin," replied the librarian, a grin upon her face. "Its pages are glued together with globs of venomous, reptilian spit."

Gilbert snorted. "Dragons don't exist."

"They do on the island of Komodo."

"Yeah, right! Where's that?"

"Look it up," the woman said, stepping back. "This is a library, after all." She rearranged a couple of novels on a nearby shelf. "You can't check out that book. But you are allowed to read it at your own risk."

Gilbert gulped. "At my own risk?"

"Silently read the words inside your head, but don't speak them if you aren't ready for the consequences. Don't read aloud what isn't allowed." With that said, the librarian turned and left Gilbert alone with the faceless book.

The book almost seemed to hiss as Gilbert opened it. Blood-red words written in nonsensical phrases filled the yellowed pages.

On one particularly worn page was a drawing of a closed mouth. A few red lines of unintelligible language were scripted beneath the image. Gilbert recognized letters from the alphabet he knew, but the words they constructed made no sense to him.

Gilbert looked around the room and found the librarian

with her back turned to him. He took a deep breath and whispered the spell aloud.

Gilbert wasn't even sure he was correctly pronouncing most of the words. But at least he was giving it a shot.

Suddenly, the librarian was in front of him. "I thought I told you not to read that aloud! Go on! Get out of here!"

Before he could exit, the woman snatched the book of spells from the boy's hands, but not before Gilbert caught one last glance at the drawing of the mouth on the page. The mouth was no longer closed. It now smiled wide, revealing rows and rows of jagged fangs between blistered lips.

Later, in Science class, Gilbert's palms itched. He did his best not to scratch. His mom had always told him scratching only made itching worse.

Gilbert raised his red right hand. Miss Walker came over and wrote Gilbert a pass to the nurse's office, if only to give herself a momentary reprieve from one of her gabbier students.

In the hallway, Gilbert looked at his left palm and discovered that he had dug a hole into his flesh with his fingernails. His heart sunk into his guts. The wound wasn't bleeding, but he knew it was only a matter of time before it gushed.

He ran to the nurse's office, not daring to look back down at his hands. Mercifully, the nurse had no other patients at the moment.

"Oh, dear." She clucked her tongue like a worried hen. "What did you do to yourself?"

"How bad is it?" Gilbert said.

And then he saw his hands. Each palm had a hole in it. The holes were the size of nickels. Neither hole bled, but he could see the tender pink flesh beneath the skin.

The nurse wrapped Gilbert's hands in gauze and sent him back to class. At Edgar Allan Poe Middle School, only the kids with broken or detached limbs were sent home.

The itching didn't stop. It only increased. Outside his

classroom door, Gilbert froze at the sound of muffled voices.

The voices didn't come from inside the classroom. No, these voices were coming from right there in front of Gilbert.

They were coming from his hands.

Gilbert took a deep breath and slowly unwrapped the gauze from his left hand. When he saw what was beneath the bandages, he nearly fainted.

The hole in his palm was larger now. Within minutes, it had somehow grown to the size of a fifty-cent piece. Only, now, the hole was a mouth. A mouth with rows and rows of fangs between its blistered lips. It kind of resembled the open jaws of a tiny shark, jagged and hungry. Made for biting and inflicting pain.

The little mouth cackled in his grasp.

Gilbert tore the gauze free of his right hand and found an identical fanged monstrosity on his other palm. This one oozed drool and flicked a black, snake-like tongue up at him. So, not a shark's mouth. But something far, far worse. Hot, rancid breath rose from behind its fangs, stinking like rotten garbage. Disgusting! Gilbert wondered if that's how his own breath smelled.

"Boo," said the right hand.

Gilbert felt faint, rubbery in the knees.

"Don't be too scared," the left hand shrieked.

The classroom door opened. Miss Walker glared at Gilbert. "Messing around in the hallway, are we?"

"Yes!" said the right hand.

"Most certainly!" offered the left.

"What was that?" Miss Walker crossed her arms.

Gilbert shoved his hands into his pants pockets. "N-Nothing," he said to the teacher. "Can I come in?"

"Only if you can quietly take the quiz."

"Yeah," said Gilbert. "I can."

"But we can't!" one of his hands squeaked from inside a pocket. The other hand giggled.

Somehow, Miss Walker didn't hear this and she allowed Gilbert into the classroom. The teacher placed the quiz in front of him and walked away.

Gilbert clenched his right hand into a fist, silencing the mouth. He freed the hand from his pocket and grabbed his pencil.

Almost immediately, the mouth began to chew on the pencil like a beaver feasting on a small tree. Wooden shavings spilled onto Gilbert's desk.

"No!" Gilbert shouted. With his left hand, he tried to snatch the pencil away from the right. But the left hand wanted a piece too, and his hands began a tug-of-war over the tool.

"Yummy!" said the left hand.

"Scrumptious!" declared the right.

"What was that, Gilbert?" fumed Miss Walker from across the room. "No talking during the exam!"

"But it's not me!" he tried to explain.

"Yes, it is," said a snooty girl sitting beside him.

Gilbert dropped the pencil to the desk and shoved his hands back inside his pockets. "I'm done."

"You didn't even start the quiz," said Miss Walker.

"I forgot to study," he said.

"Idiot," a hand snickered.

"Dummy," offered the other.

Gilbert slumped down in his seat, and, for once, had nothing more to say.

"I'm so disappointed in you," his mom said at the dinner table that evening. "Do you *want* to go to military school?"

Behind a full plate of spaghetti and meatballs, Gilbert shook his head. "No, I don't."

"Two teachers called me at work today! Two!" Her eyes fired lasers at his face. "They both said you were making voices in class? Now, why would you do that?"

"It wasn't me," said Gilbert.

"It was me!" said the hand in his left pocket.

"And me, too!" added the hand in the right. The fanged holes had chewed through his pants pockets and had been biting at his legs for hours.

His mom's face was tomato red. "You just can't help yourself, can you? I don't appreciate the ventriloquist act, so you go upstairs."

Gilbert didn't even bother to fight back. He trudged upstairs, his belly rumbling.

As he closed his bedroom door behind him, his right hand tried to gnaw on the brass doorknob. He smacked the hand across the mouth, and it snapped at his left middle finger, drawing blood.

The blood from Gilbert's bit finger trickled down into his palm. The left mouth darted a dark tongue to the blood, lapping it up like a vampire bat.

"Mmmm, better than pencil," said the left hand.

"I want some," said the right mouth.

"ShutupshutupshutupshutupSHUTUP!" Gilbert screamed, his cheeks wet, but the loud mouths merely laughed at him.

Gilbert reached under his bed, where his right hand attempted to devour a spider in a single bite. After a few seconds, he found what he was looking for.

Despite the protests from the chomping mouths, Gilbert managed to slide a pair of thick snow gloves over his hands. He then took out his old mp3 player, placed headphones over his ears, and listened to his favorite tunes at full blast.

At least he drowned out the noisy hands for the rest of the night.

The next morning, Gilbert wore the snow gloves to school. His Math and Art teachers made him remove them during class. His hands spoke freely.

He realized that clapping his hands together seemed to stun the mouths into silence. But, when they came to, the mouths spoke louder than before.

After second period, Gilbert went to his English class. There, he showed his palms to Mr. B, a teacher who at least tried to understand kids before biting their heads off.

"It's sad to say," said Mr. B, "but these mouths aren't even the strangest things I've seen at this school."

"Can you help me?" Gilbert pleaded. "They're driving me crazy!"

"Let's go to the library together," the teacher suggested. "See if we can't get this sorted out there."

Once in the library, Mr. B said to Gilbert, "Show me the book of spells. There must be a way to remedy this."

Gilbert took the teacher to the correct shelf. He sighed in relief when he saw that the book still sat there, as if waiting for him. Mr. B opened the book and read a few pages.

"Do you understand it?" Gilbert asked, hope rising within him like floodwaters.

"Not at all," Mr. B said.

"So I'm going to be like this forever?"

"I have a plan. It might not work, but if you are willing to give it a shot . . ."

"No way, Jose," said the right hand.

"I'm staying right here," replied the left.

"Yes!" said Gilbert. "Please! Anything!"

"Very well," said Mr. B.

The teacher wrote some sort of message on a piece of paper and handed it to Gilbert. On it, the teacher had copied the spell, *but he had written each word backwards.*

"Read it aloud," the teacher instructed. "You'll hopefully be able to pronounce the words correctly this time. The curse should be reversed."

"It won't work," taunted the right hand.

"A failure, for sure," agreed the left.

"Read slowly," said Mr. B. "Carefully."

And Gilbert did. He did his best to ignore the mouths. He read more carefully than he had ever read anything before in his life.

Gilbert looked at his palms. "I don't think it worked."

Suddenly, Gilbert's legs turned to jelly. The room spun. His vision blurred. He collapsed against a bookshelf, nearly bringing it down upon him.

Mr. B caught his student. "I'm taking you to the nurse, Gilbert."

"Wait," said the boy. Gilbert stood tall and strong. "They're gone, Mr. B. They're *gone!*"

He showed his palms to the teacher. The mouths had vanished. Mr. B smiled wide and gave the boy a high five.

"Thanks," Gilbert said. "I'm going to go get a snack before the bell rings. I haven't eaten in over a day."

"Good," said a low voice. "I'm starving."

Mr. B scratched his head. "Who said that?"

Gilbert's spine tingled. He lifted his T-shirt and screamed.

"I'm hungry," complained a gaping mouth in Gilbert's stomach. "Feed me now."

YOU BREAK, YOU BYE-BYE

STEVEN KNEW PRINCESS HOLMES was no princess. Sure, she often wore a regal smile, and she always dressed like royalty, but the only title she possibly held was "the Queen of Mean." Nonetheless, she was very popular and very pretty.

It was no secret that hanging around Princess could be dangerous to one's emotional health, but her popularity was often contagious. If Princess "liked" a person, chances were other important people at school would, too.

That is why relatively unpopular Steven dared approach the girl in the hallway after school one day. Princess and her bestie, Sabrina, were laughing about a classmate's ugly shoes when the nervous boy cleared his throat behind them.

The girls turned to the nerd. "What are you staring at?" Princess snapped.

"Hey, Princess," Steven said. "I was wondering if I could speak to you privately?"

"Why? You gonna do my homework if I do?"

Sabrina snorted and said, "I wouldn't let him do that. He looks like a geek, but my grades are better than his."

"Maybe *you* should do my homework, then?" Princess

proposed.

"No, thanks." Sabrina lowered her head and took some steps back.

Princess eyed Steven. "What is it?"

"Do you have a new boyfriend yet?" Steven asked.

Princess looked back at eavesdropping Sabrina. Both girls giggled.

"No," said Princess. "You're interested?"

Steven nodded. "Who wouldn't be?"

"Good point."

"I mean, I know we don't talk much—"

Princess rolled her eyes. "Or ever."

"—but I'm a nice guy, and I've admired you from afar for a really, really long time."

"Is that right?"

"That means he's obsessed with you!" Sabrina offered.

"Are you obsessed with me?" Princess asked Steven.

He shook his head. "I mean, I just like you a lot." He took a slender jewelry box from his sweatshirt pocket.

"What's that?" said Princess.

"A gift for you." Steven handed the box over into her waiting hands. "I hope you like it."

"This box looks old and faded."

Sabrina rushed to Princess's side. "Open it already!"

Princess flipped open the jewelry box. Inside lay a glass heart pendant on a silver chain.

"It's a family heirloom," Steven explained. "My grandma wore it. My mom wore it . . ."

"Ew," said Sabrina. "It's used."

"That's okay." Princess smiled. "I like it."

"Great!" Steven pumped a fist. "Be careful with it, though. It's very delicate."

Princess gave him a hug. "I promise to take really good care of it." She was thin and bony. Kind of frail, like a baby bird.

"So, am I your boyfriend now?"

Princess broke away. "Can I hold on to this necklace and think about it?"

"Yeah, for sure!" Steven smiled happily. "Bye, Princess. See you later." The boy ran off, probably late for the bus.

Sabrina said, "He's a loser, right?"

"Totally," Princess agreed. Together they laughed. "Try on the necklace."

Princess pulled the piece of jewelry from the box. "It's so *hideous*," she said. "*You* wear it."

She tossed the necklace to Sabrina. The bestie caught it and gave it a closer inspection.

"Gross." She tossed it back to Princess.

The girls threw the necklace back and forth, back and forth like a hot potato. Sabrina let the necklace fly higher than it had before . . . and Princess let it crash against the linoleum floor.

The heart shattered as it hit the ground. The silver chain tangled around shards of glass like a dead worm.

For an instant, Princess thought back to the car accident two years ago.

Hanging upside down by a taut seatbelt, Princess had, at first, been dizzy and confused in the backseat. Until she saw window glass scattered all around the vehicle's interior and out in the road, she had trouble remembering where she even was.

And then she saw Mom, too: a rag doll, unmoving, at the steering wheel.

"Whoops," said Sabrina.

"Yeah." Princess wiped her eyes. Rolled them. "Big whoops."

The girls walked off, leaving the broken necklace for the custodian to sweep away.

Hours later, Princess stood on the staircase at home. "Whatever, Dad." She waved a dismissive hand to her father, who stood at the bottom of the steps. "I'm here now, safe and sound."

"You need to be home by five o'clock on a school night," Dad scolded. "How many times do we need to have this conversation?"

"A lot?" said Princess.

"Do you really want to speak to me that way? What would your mother think if she was looking down at us right now?"

Dad did this often. Used the Mom Card. Implied that the dead woman might be watching Princess's every move from Heaven. Shaking her celestial head in disappointment. Judging.

Whenever Dad dealt the card, Princess saw it as a cheap shot. A tactic used to weaken her defenses.

But Princess refused to be weak. That's what everyone expects of you when your parent dies: weakness. And then they take advantage of you. Weaken you even more.

Princess Holmes was a redwood tree. Powerful. Resilient. Strong.

Not some little flower easily bent by other's words, no matter how truthful they might be.

She was the bender. Not the other way around.

She was the one firing lethal barbs, always striking first and catching others off-guard. Confusing them, flustering them. Making them weak instead of her.

If people backpedaled because of Princess, they couldn't successfully jab at her or put any dents in her armor.

So, even though she hoped it wasn't true, Princess said to her father, "Mom's not up there. Nobody's watching."

After staring at his daughter for a few seconds and shaking his head, Dad replied, "Maybe this will affect you more, then. If you're late one more time, I'm going to take away your phone. All of your electronics. Do you hear me?"

Dad knew how to get his jabs in, after all.

Ever since Mom's death, he'd given Princess everything she'd desired. And more. Princess didn't need that gift train to stop rolling into town.

She said, "Hear you, loud and clear," and grinned. "I'm sorry, okay? I promise I'll listen to you next time."

She jogged up the rest of the stairs, humming to herself, drowning out the last of her father's words. She darted into her bedroom and slammed the door shut behind her.

At the doorway, Princess let some tears fall.

What if Mom *was* watching? What *would* she think?

Would she be proud of her daughter's toughness in the aftermath of the accident? Be proud of the way Princess handled herself over the past couple of years?

Probably not.

No, no, no! Princess had to get her mind elsewhere, someplace happier, where she was in control.

She threw her backpack onto the floor and wandered over to a pair of pink speakers. She plugged in her phone and turned on the device. She found her favorite song and pressed "play."

Exactly six seconds of the song played, then a low, droning buzz spilled from the speakers. Puzzled, Princess picked up the phone.

A series of dark scribbles zigged and zagged across its small screen. Princess jabbed at the machine's buttons. She even turned it off and on a few times.

Her brand-new phone was already dead.

Princess groaned and hurled the apparatus across the room. It knocked over a framed photograph of her and a smiling Sabrina.

Dad was *so* buying her another phone tomorrow!

Princess didn't bother to pick up the photo. Instead, she hopped into the seat in front of her purple laptop. This was her personal throne, where most of her awesome ideas originated from.

Within a minute, the laptop was on and connected to the Internet. Two minutes after that, Princess was in the middle of five separate conversations on Faboo Instant Messenger.

On their way to Sabrina's house, Princess had learned a juicy little secret. Sabrina had a killer crush on Ruben, a beautiful boy Princess had dated for a few weeks last year in sixth grade.

Princess had pretended to be okay with it, but in reality she still had feelings for Ruben herself. If she couldn't have him, no one could.

Princess was telling her Faboo friends all about Sabrina's secret when her bestie entered the website.

Sabrina: hi
Princess: lol
Sabrina: ya??
Princess: rofl
Sabrina: wats sooooo funny??
Princess: i just saw u
Sabrina: o ya! lol! wats nu?? rofl
Princess: nutin
Sabrina: ya im bored
Princess: my dad yelled at me again! lol
Sabrina: xciting. y??
Princess: cuz i wuz not herr by 5! lol
Sabrina: lol ur bad
Princess: i no. im da best
Sabrina: hey can u promise??
Princess: wat?
Sabrina: ruben. i dont want ppl 2 no
Princess: of course. ur secret iz safe wit me
Sabrina: just promise?? plz??
Princess: i promise
Sabrina: u R da best!!
Princess: u no it! jk
Sabrina: no ur not! rofl
Princess: ya ur rite. im

The laptop screen suddenly went dark.

Princess smacked the side of the computer. She checked to see if she had accidentally unplugged it, then she remembered fully charging it that morning.

"What the—?!"

She rose from her throne, stormed across the room, and wrapped a hand around the doorknob.

"Dad!" Princess shrieked as she flung open her door. "DAAAAAAAAAAAAD! WE HAVE AN EMERGENCY!"

The next day during Health, Mr. West walked around the classroom, handing back graded papers to students. When he reached Princess, the teacher said, "You know, your grade can't improve if you don't ever turn anything in."

"Okay."

"What's due tomorrow?"

Princess sighed. "The homework?"

"Which is . . . ?"

"Two paragraphs about what I need to read in the textbook tonight."

"Which pages are those?"

"Pages 113 to 131."

"Exactly," said Mr. West. "Glad to see you're paying attention."

"I'll do it tonight," Princess insisted. "I promise."

"Very good. I hope you do." The teacher moved on to another student.

Under her breath, Princess added, "You wish."

There was a quick creak, and, before she knew it, she had tumbled to the floor and was staring at a classmate's scruffy sneakers.

Almost the entire class roared with laughter. Her cheeks burned bright. Even her yelling at them from the floor to shut up did nothing to calm the students down.

Princess almost cried. But she'd never give others the satisfaction of seeing her be vulnerable.

A helping hand appeared before her. Princess looked up at stupid Steven. She swatted his hand away and scrambled to her feet.

"Okay . . ." said the boy. "So, hey, real quick: you're not wearing the necklace I gave you. You don't like it?"

Princess huffed, turned away from Steven, and glared at her teacher. "I need a new seat. NOW!"

⊚ ⊚ ⊚

The next period was P.E., and Princess was not surprised to find Sabrina waiting for her by the locker room entrance. Princess smirked.

"Why?" Sabrina said, teary eyed. "Why did you lie to me?"

"I don't really know," said Princess. It was the truth, too.

"You promised! Now everyone knows!"

"Everybody doesn't know." But they really did.

"I can't trust you, Princess. Why did you do this to me? You're a ... such a ..." Sabrina broke into sobs.

"I'm your bestie," Princess said, collecting her friend into a gentle hug. "And I'm sorry I hurt your feelings. Honestly. I was wrong."

"Yes, you were." Sabrina cried into Princess's shoulder.

"I'll make it all better," Princess said, patting Sabrina's back. "I promise."

But twenty minutes later, Princess found herself on the P.E. field spreading a vicious rumor about her best friend.

Sabrina didn't get to stand up to Princess without being put back into her place. Princess was the one in charge around here! Nobody challenged her and got away with it!

"Sabrina kisses her pillow every night before she goes to bed," Princess told an eighth-grader named Melanie.

"She pretends it's Ruben's face, 'cause she thinks kissing the pillow will make her dream about him while she sleeps."

"Wow." Melanie laughed. "That's just sad."

"Yeah," said Princess. "You gotta tell every—"

THWACK!

A soccer ball rocketed through the air and smacked Princess in the face. Blood spurted from her crushed nose.

Princess dropped to her knees, screaming like she had never screamed before. Tears bit at the corners of her eyes. The fire at the center of her face grew hotter with each passing second.

Finally, the pain engulfed her. Princess passed out.

When she awoke, Princess was strapped to a gurney in the back of a speeding ambulance. Her neck was in a foam brace. Her eyesight was blurred with tears.

Her nose, however, hurt less. The paramedic leaning over her must have given her some type of medicine.

"Hey, there," said the man. "We're almost to the hospital. You're going to be fine."

Princess nodded, trying to appear strong, but inside she was beyond scared. She hated hospitals. The last time she was in a hospital, Mom had been on life support. That didn't end well.

"You're Princess," the young paramedic said. It was a statement, not a question.

Did she know this guy? Where had she seen him before?

"You know my brother, Steven Grace, right? He gave you a necklace yesterday?"

Oh, great. Just her luck!

Princess did her best to shake her head, no.

"Yeah, Steven. My little bro."

Princess shook her head again.

"There's another girl at your school named Princess? Really?"

Her eyes lit up. "Yes," she said. "It wasn't me. I promise."

The paramedic stared at her for a good, long while. Did he believe her? Was he mad about the necklace? Could he tell she was lying?

"Huh." He shrugged. "Weird. Because Steven didn't have permission to give the necklace away. And I really want it returned, because it's protected by one of our great-grandmother's spells, and bad things could happen if it—Hey, you know what? If you're the wrong Princess, I guess none of this concerns you."

She giggled inside her head. Yes! He actually believed her! What an idi—

"No!" a deep voice shouted from the front of the ambulance. "No, no, NO! The brakes aren't working! They aren't WORKING! HOLD ON! HOLD—!"

Princess's heart leapt into her throat as a thunderous crash filled her ears. She soared through the air, and everything faded to black once more.

A headline in the next morning's newspaper read:

"POPULAR MIDDLE SCHOOL STUDENT KILLED IN AMBULANCE CRASH"

Steven shook his head in disbelief as he read the article. He was in the hospital, at his brother's bedside. Derek had a broken collarbone and a shattered left femur, but, aside from that, the paramedic was fine. So was the ambulance's driver, Julian, who had suffered a few broken ribs and fingers.

"Lucky," Steven said softly while he watched his sibling sleep.

Sure, now Princess Holmes would be a name no one ever forgot, but this time it would definitely be for all the wrong reasons. She would always be the most popular dead girl at Edgar Allan Poe Middle School.

IT'S A ZOO IN THERE

THE SEVENTH-GRADERS IN MRS. Perez's fourth period English class were animals. They threw objects at each other, and sometimes even at the teacher. The students didn't like to stay in their seats, and they always talked. Room 172 was rarely quiet, and every other word out of a kid's mouth seemed more suited to an R-rated movie than to a classroom.

Sometimes the misbehavior made Xavier chuckle under his breath, but more often than not it caused him to shake his head in disapproval and disbelief. He and his friends never dared to act in such a way. They had respect for themselves, their school, and *most* of their teachers.

Xavier was an eighth-grader. He had worked very hard for two years to get to where he was now. Only the very best students were offered the opportunity to be a T.A., or teacher's assistant.

Instead of taking an elective course, Xavier assisted Mrs. Perez for a single class period every day, doing anything he could that would help relieve her of the stress he constantly saw on her face. He graded spelling tests, organized bulletin boards, ran errands to other classrooms—and, almost daily, escorted a disrespectful student to the principal's office.

Whenever Mrs. Perez knew she would be absent, she made sure to ask Xavier ahead of time to assist the substitute teacher. So it was no surprise when the latest substitute, Mr. Guest, called Xavier over to the teacher's desk eleven minutes into fourth period.

"Are the kids always like this?" Mr. Guest asked, gesturing to the seventh-graders eating candy and tossing it around the room.

Xavier nodded. "Pretty much. You have to be 'stern' with them. That's what Mrs. Perez says."

Mr. Guest frowned, scratching his bald head. "I thought I had heard better things about this school? It's the only reason I took the job—but *all* her classes are like this."

Xavier shrugged. "You know how kids act sometimes when subs are around."

"Well," said Mr. Guest, "I tend to work high schools. And they're nothing like *this*."

Xavier didn't know what to say, so he said nothing.

The sub sighed, rubbing his eyes. "I don't suppose you have anything for my headache, do you?"

"Um . . ." Xavier shook his head.

"Of course not." Mr. Guest lifted a piece of paper from the desk. "According to this lesson plan, I'm supposed to review metaphors with the class for Friday's test."

Xavier said, "Yeah, I guess."

"I've done that with three other classes already. I'm looking for a little break here, Xavier."

"Okay . . ."

"Do you know where she keeps the videos? I see there's a T.V. over there, but I can't find the videos anywhere."

Mr. Guest pointed to a dusty television in the back of the classroom. It sat atop a rusted cart and was practically buried beneath old worksheets Mrs. Perez had yet to file.

Xavier said, "That thing's old. It only takes VHS."

"Yeah," said the teacher. "So where are the videotapes?"

When Xavier hesitated, Mr. Guest leaned in so close that

Xavier could smell coffee on the man's breath. "Come on, now. I'm asking for your help here. *Man-to-man.* Where are the videos kept?"

Xavier backed up a couple of steps. "Sorry, I don't know. Honestly." And it was the truth. Mrs. Perez never showed videos in class, much to the displeasure of her excessively whiny students.

"Fine." Mr. Guest was angry now. "Go sit back down."

Xavier happily made his way back to his desk, off to one side of the room. Sneaky little Ricky stood next to it, his hand inside Xavier's backpack.

"Hey, get out of there!"

"I was looking for … um …" Ricky smiled. "For a pencil, man. So, you got one?"

Xavier tore the backpack from Ricky's grubby hands. "You little rat, sit down or I'm telling Mrs. Perez tomorrow."

"Ooooooooh, I'm so scared," Ricky said. But he walked off.

Suddenly, Mr. Guest shouted, "SIT DOWN AND SHUT UP!"

Xavier sat and shut up. The rest of the room fell silent, as well.

The substitute teacher sneered.

"For the next thirty-nine minutes, we're going to be talking about metaphors. That's what your teacher wants us to do, so get in your seats and pay attention to me."

Students who stood remained standing. Those who had been talking began to giggle.

"This is *not* how the rest of the class period will go," Mr. Guest boomed. "I have a seating chart right here with each of your names on it, so I suggest you start showing better behavior."

The man's face was an unhealthy maroon hue. Perhaps Xavier shouldn't have told him to be "stern." He looked close to a heart attack.

Aside from some whispers, the classroom was quiet. "That's better," said Mr. Guest, more calmly. "Let's first review the definition of a metaphor. Who here can raise a hand and define 'metaphor' for the class?"

Charles raised his hand, which surprised Xavier. Charles was notorious for shouting out at any given opportunity.

Mr. Guest examined the seating chart. "Yes, Charles? You have a definition?"

"Your head," said the boy. "Your big, bald head is as shiny as a bowling ball."

The classroom erupted in laughter. Mr. Guest's face was a crimson balloon about to pop.

"Hey, teacher," said Vanessa, one of the mouthiest girls Xavier had ever met. "I got a definition."

Mr. Guest didn't even reply. He merely glared.

Vanessa said, "The substitute teacher is fatter than an elephant."

Kids almost fell to the floor laughing. Xavier held his face in his hands, trying to hide from the nuclear meltdown building up inside Mr. Guest. It took all of Xavier's strength to look through his fingertips at the sub.

Strangely, the next words out of the man's mouth weren't mean-spirited. "No, I'm sorry," Mr. Guest said quietly. "Those aren't definitions, class. Those are *examples*." He paused. "And they're actually examples of *similes*. I asked you what a *metaphor* was, not a *simile*."

"We don't care!" Grant said while he leaned over to his friend, Austin, and punched him in the shoulder.

"A metaphor is used when you compare two nouns without using the words 'like,' 'as,' 'resembles' or 'than.'" Mr. Guest actually grinned. "Allow me now to give *you* some examples."

Xavier almost mentioned that similes were technically metaphors too, even if they used "like," "as," "resembles," or "than." His current English teacher, Mrs. Aranda, had taught him that. But Xavier didn't mention anything to Mr. Guest about his mistake. He didn't want to erase the teacher's smile from his face.

Mr. Guest removed a pad of yellow sticky notes from a drawer in Mrs. Perez's desk. With a pen, he quickly scribbled something onto the pad. He removed the top sticky note and walked toward Grant.

"Grant," said Mr. Guest.

The large boy slumped into his seat. Grant groaned. "What do you want?"

"Pay attention, class," said Mr. Guest. "Grant *is* a gruesome grizzly who can't keep his meaty paws to himself."

The teacher secured the sticky note to Grant's forehead. In large, bold letters, the word, "GRIZZLY," now hung from the boy's face.

Mr. Guest wrote a word on the next sticky note and placed it onto Vanessa's cheek: "VIPER."

Mr. Guest said, "Vanessa *is* a viper whose venomous words poison each room in which she slithers."

Sergio was labeled "SEAL."

The sub said, "Sergio *is* a seal darting under and over desks like they're floating chunks of ice."

Xavier was shocked. The students were actually paying attention. They seemed to be enjoying the activity. Some begged for Mr. Guest to label them a specific beast like "LION," "TIGER," or "BEAR."

Maybe the man actually knew what he was doing.

Ten minutes later, the entire class had been labeled. Xavier had politely refused the offer to participate in the activity. The sticky notes were back in the drawer.

Mr. Guest stood at the front of the room grinning, his face its normal complexion.

Then, "CROCODILE" Charles removed his sticky note. He balled it up and threw it like a rocket at "FERRET" Francela. She didn't appreciate that, so she crumpled her label and threw it back at Charles. Only, she hit "EEL" Evelyn instead.

Just like that, the Great Sticky Note War of 172 began.

Mr. Guest stood in the middle of it all, jaw dropped. He shook his head while gutsier students pelted him with their labels. The look on his face seemed to say, *What have I done?*

Xavier stood from his seat. He figured the broom and dustpan would come in handy very soon.

"ANIMALS!" the substitute screamed. "YOU'RE ANIMALS! ALL OF YOU!"

A wild, maniacal laugh suddenly drowned out everything else. "HYENA" Henry had apparently lost his mind.

"GORILLA" Grayson growled at Henry to shut his mouth. Literally, the hulking boy *growled*. No words were spoken.

"JACKAL" Julia didn't like Grayson threatening her boyfriend. She leapt onto her desk, yapping at the gorilla. She bared her teeth, salivating like a rabid dog. She tackled Grayson and bit into his throat.

Within seconds, the classroom was a jungle, with students darting and jumping around on all-fours. Desks were toppled and thrown. Shrieks, growls, howls, screeches, and roars echoed off the walls.

The animals were loose, angry, and hungry. Hair and flesh ripped. Blood spilled.

Xavier had the supply closet open. He grabbed the broom just as something latched onto his back and bit the nape of his neck.

Xavier cried out in pain, throwing little "RAT" Ricky to the ground. The seething seventh-grader scurried back toward the T.A. Xavier smacked him in the face and ribs with the bristly end of the broom.

Then, "COUGAR" Colin pounced on the rat, and Xavier turned away from Ricky's horrifying cries.

At the front of the room, Mr. Guest was cornered by a grizzly and a viper. He shouted, "Stay back!" to Grant and Vanessa, but it was the teacher who needed help. Grant's hands were drenched in blood not his own, and gore dripped from Vanessa's lips.

Xavier dodged an owl's talons. With the broom handle, he swatted away a torpedo-like shark.

Xavier was almost to Mr. Guest. The substitute teacher had already crumpled to the classroom floor. He hadn't been attacked yet. He'd passed out from fear. The grizzly and viper sniffed the unconscious man.

"Grant!" Xavier shouted. "Vanessa! Leave him alone!" But the boy and girl were no longer there.

The bear bellowed and lunged downward. The viper hissed and dove in, as well.

Mr. Guest screamed as he was eaten alive.

Each animal bit into an opposite side of the teacher's face, peeling it apart in unison. Mr. Guest's exposed jaws shrieked in agony. Because the man's cheeks were now gone, Xavier could see the guy's tongue flopping around inside his mouth like a fish trapped on land.

Mr. Guest finally fell silent after the grizzly swiped powerfully at his neck. The teacher's Adam's apple smacked wetly onto the floor and rolled haphazardly across the room, ricocheting off of some table legs.

Stunned, Xavier stood frozen against Mrs. Perez's desk, trying unsuccessfully to ignore the substitute's gurgles and the grizzly's crunches. Now Xavier was a target again. "SHARK" Stefanie circled back toward him for a second attack. "LEOPARD" Leonel was also approaching on the prowl.

Desperate, Xavier threw open the desk drawer containing the sticky notes. He had no pen, no pencil. The shark was close. The leopard was closer.

Xavier pressed two fingers to the back of his injured neck. With his bloody fingers, he painted a word onto the note pad and stuck the sticky note to his chest.

He roared, "I AM A T-REX STOMPING THROUGH THIS PREHISTORIC WASTELAND! GET OUT OF MY WAY OR SUFFER MY WRATH!"

The shark retreated. The leopard slunk back into the shadows.

Xavier dropped the broom. Indeed, he felt stronger and taller somehow. *Much stronger. Much taller.*

He was hungry. Angry. Powerful.

He held out his arms in front of his chest and hooked his

fingers into claws. His teeth suddenly felt sharper against his tongue. His mouth began to salivate at the thought of eating fresh meat.

Xavier was a monster, ready to explode with rage.

But some small part of him told him to move forward. Get out of that room. Find help.

He stomped a path through the destroyed classroom. The other animals gave him wide berth, cowering and growling at him from a distance.

But as he neared the door, his steps grew difficult and stilted. Each second, he found he moved slower . . . slower . . .

The T.A. had made the wrong choice: *Tyrannosaurus rex* had no place in this day and age.

Xavier's bones were fossilizing within his dinosaur body.

A couple of the carnivores noticed his slow pace, his sudden weakness. The bloodthirsty beasts coiled their muscles for attack. A wolverine and a jaguar simultaneously leapt for the lizard king.

They tackled the dinosaur to the floor. Clawing. Biting. Xavier roared, using all his strength to kick at and push away the creatures as they aimed for his throat.

He caught the wolverine in the ribs with his foot, launching it against a wall. Bone cracked. The beast slid limply to the ground.

The jaguar was still a blur, wild with hunger, while the *tyrannosaur's* energy was nearly extinct. His neck was vulnerable. Exposed.

Xavier had the strength to try one last defense. He growled:

"I AM A TRAIN, A POWERFUL STEEL LOCOMO-TIVE THAT CANNOT BE STOPPED BY ANY ANIMAL!"

Immediately, warmth bloomed inside Xavier's chest like a heap of burning coal. A fire raged, melting all feelings of petrification away from his extremities.

Heat rose from his body, driving the jaguar back a few steps. The animal snarled in a moment of fear.

Standing confidently again, Xavier stared down the feline.

Steam billowed from Xavier's flaring nostrils. He felt like an indestructible piece of machinery.

The jaguar, feeling indestructible itself, sprung for the boy, attempting to slice Xavier to ribbons. But it bent back its claws instead. It broke its teeth on Xavier's hardened exterior. The big cat jumped away, yowling in pain and confusion.

With renewed vigor, Xavier surged forward, not once looking back. He focused on the door, on his route. Zooming forward, forward, forward.

He smashed through the closed classroom door, nearly ripping it from its hinges. He stormed into the hallway screeching, "CHOO-CHOO! CHOO-CHOO!"

Up ahead, two school security guards raced in his direction. Xavier collapsed, out of steam, then almost immediately felt himself returning to normal.

Outside the classroom, Xavier was once again Xavier.

A security guard knelt by his side. "Are you okay? We'll get the nurse over here as soon as poss—"

"Hey!" the other guard yelled. "We have to get the rest of these kids out of here!" He stood staring through the doorway he had just yanked open.

Inside, half a dozen bodies were motionless on the floor. They practically floated in puddles of spilled blood. Red claw marks streaked across desktops and walls. Various limbs had been severed from their hosts and dripped like fresh roadkill. Lifeless eyes gazed out into the hall, no longer seeing the horrors playing out around them.

Surviving students slashed, dashed, howled, and yowled in frenzy around the space. Ragged pieces of flesh dangled from between their teeth.

"Just be careful," Xavier warned the guard. "It's a zoo in there."

THE BLACK CAT 2.0

T'HE SHRILL CRY OF an animal in distress echoed throughout an otherwise lifeless hallway. The space was flanked on both sides by rusty lockers and pieces of discarded refuse.

Grant, just released from his usual after-school detention in Mr. Huntley's History class, walked alone past the closed library, on his way to the front gate. But the familiar animal wail froze him in his tracks.

Somewhere nearby was a cat, either wounded or in trouble of another kind. Grant knew the sound well. His cat, Pluto, ironically named after a favorite canine cartoon character, had made a similar racket whenever Grant had played with him.

The seventh-grader turned his head, silenced his breathing, and listened as hard as he could. Where was the cat? Why couldn't he see it, pinpoint its location?

Grant took small but deliberate steps in what he thought was the right direction. Sure enough, the cat's cries grew louder, louder still.

Soon, Grant realized the animal was inside a locker. Locker A256, to be exact.

The boy spoke to the cat through the door. "How'd you get

in there?"

All around school, abandoned lockers lined the school's hallways like forgotten memories. Sure, Grant had tagged a few with permanent marker, but they had no other use, because it was impossible to open them. The administration hadn't assigned lockers to students in years: something about there being too many kids nowadays, or students taking too much time between classes to fetch their books.

The cat yowled. The boy put his face against the horizontal slits in the locker door. A single yellow eye peered back at him from the darkness.

Grant grinned. "How do you like it in there, pal?" He slammed his palms against the locker door, further frightening the trapped animal.

The boy laughed.

He didn't know the combination but spun the locker's dial anyway, stopping on three random numbers. Then he pushed up on the locker handle. To his surprise, the door swung open.

"Whoa! No way!" The boy felt like a genius. Well, super lucky, at least.

He gazed inside the locker and gasped.

The cat was black, with mangy fur. It was frail, thin, and had a single golden eye. The other side of its face displayed a vacant socket, home only to a sliver of pink flesh visible beneath a drooping lid.

"P-Pluto?"

Grant couldn't believe it. Pluto? But ... But how? Pluto was dead! Just thirteen days earlier, Grant had tied the old cat down with a belt, taken the switchblade he stole from his cousin Brian, and ... and—

The cat hissed and swiped at him with a claw. No, this wasn't Pluto. This cat was a fighter. Plus, it had a slash of white fur on its neck. Pluto had been endless midnight. This cat was just an impostor. Close, but not close enough. Pluto 2.0.

Grant's heartbeat slowed.

The cat leapt out of the locker and darted down the hall, around the corner, out of sight.

Definitely not Pluto. Grant's cat had been sickly and slow. Easy to catch. Easy to hold down. Easy to slice.

The boy shrugged. Finding the cat like that had certainly been weird, but he didn't want to dwell on it. He wasn't a detective. If anything, he wanted to shake the hand of the kid who had somehow forced Pluto 2.0 inside the locker in the first place.

Grant closed the locker door, lifting its handle once more, just in case. It swung open again.

"Broken," he said, smiling wide. He slipped two heavy textbooks inside the locker and closed it.

This was a discovery he'd like to keep to himself. He decided right then and there that Locker A256 was now his and his alone.

Minutes later, Grant walked alongside Gulf Avenue, looking over his shoulder. Wherever he traveled outside of school, the boy had to be aware of his surroundings. He had big fists and a bigger mouth, all of which had made him wildly unpopular. He had to be sure the older brothers or cousins of kids he bullied weren't waiting in the shadows or around some corner for him, ready for revenge.

Up ahead, half of a block away, a rose-colored car pulled away from the curb and drove toward him. The vehicle's frame hung low to the ground and its windows were tinted.

Grant gulped. Someone was coming for him. Likely a carload of somebodies, eager to leap out and attack him like ravenous piranha.

He slung his backpack around to his front and unzipped the smaller pouch. His clammy hand reached inside and fumbled for his stolen knife.

The car was closer to Grant now, closer still. Its engine revved, the heart of a hungry beast.

A drive-by, Grant suddenly thought. Just like in the movies or on the ten o'clock news. So this was how they were going to take him out.

Grant's fingers found the blade's handle just as the car moved on, racing off to some other destination, its inhabitants completely uninterested in the lone boy on the sidewalk.

Relieved, Grant let out a deep breath, released the knife, and wiped sweat from his brow. A false alarm was always appreciated. He swung the backpack back around.

Behind him, the boy heard another car moving down the street. He turned to see a minivan driven by a woman about his mom's age—or the age she would have been, if she were still around.

Then he spotted Pluto 2.0 standing across the street, as if appearing out of thin air. The black cat momentarily locked eyes with Grant and then zoomed into the middle of Gulf Avenue, directly in front of the van.

The woman behind the wheel reacted quickly, swerving to avoid the foolish feline. She missed smearing the cat's guts across the asphalt by mere inches. The van's front left tire, however, dipped into a pothole and pitched the vehicle forward at an awkward angle, like a blind, bucking bronco.

Grant jumped back as the minivan hopped over the curb next to him, soaring through the spot where he had just stood. Falling to the ground, Grant felt the heat of the van's grill as it passed him by, the whoosh of the massive metal carriage as it missed him by inches.

With a deafening crash, the van slammed full-force into a wrought-iron fence.

Shaken, Grant rose to his feet. He had almost been pancaked! The van's dazed driver pulled away from a deployed airbag. The vehicle's windshield was cracked down its center, and its front end was a misshapen accordion.

A man ran out of a nearby house to assist the woman. He asked Grant to stay put, but Grant turned away from the scene, ignoring him.

The boy briefly searched the area for the black cat. It had

vanished, and Grant had the idea that he would do the same.

He sprinted home, a little bruised and bloody, but not really much worse for wear.

Back home, Grant quietly entered through the front door. The living room was dark, the air acrid and smoky. Dad was passed out on the couch next to a couple of empty beer bottles and a too-loud television set.

The boy quietly walked past the familiar scene, cautious not to stir the sleeping giant. Dad was no fun when awakened from an afternoon nap.

Grant made it inside his bedroom and then shut the door behind him. He threw his backpack to the floor, next to the tarantula terrarium.

Petey, his pet spider, sat still against one corner of the cage. Gordy the gecko still stuck high against the glass, near the top of the covered box.

"Good, Petey," said Grant. "I haven't missed the main event."

Grant loved animals. When he grew bored, he played games with the little critters. The boy knew most people wouldn't understand the way he played, so he kept it to himself.

His father, for example, was completely oblivious to it. The man had his mind on things more important than his son, and Grant knew it. But that was fine with the boy, because he always had his animals.

The game with Petey and Gordy had been going on for over a week now. Grant had put the gecko inside the terrarium to see how long he would last with a starving spider. The boy had intentionally left Petey unfed, hoping to force the spider after the lizard. No such luck yet.

Andre the pigeon cooed loudly in his cage beside the closet. Grant knew the bird was stressed after being snatched from the park where he had previously lived. Many of his feathers had fallen off. To even out the bird's look, Grant had plucked out a few more feathers by hand. When the pigeon had pecked at him,

Grant was forced to twist one of the bird's legs out of place.

"Hi, Andre," said the boy, raking his untrimmed fingernails against the wire cage.

The bird backed away from Grant, not looking at him.

"If you keep ignoring me, bird," said Grant, "it's shoebox time for you." Beneath his bed, Grant had a few boxes filled with tiny bones.

The pigeon looked past the boy, unfurled his wings and raised a few inches off the cage's filthy bottom, then slammed his body against the walls of his miniature prison.

Grant turned. No wonder the bird was so excited.

There was the black cat again, this time on the other side of the closed bedroom window, a paw pressed against the glass.

Grant realized the cat must have been desperate for a friend if it had followed him all the way home from school. Even though it had nearly gotten him killed, the furry jerk expected Grant to welcome it with open arms.

Not a chance.

Grant knelt down next to his backpack and unzipped the front pocket. He pulled out the knife, for a moment admiring how it looked in his hand.

In the terrarium, the tarantula was now beneath the gecko, reaching up for the reptile with two legs, waiting with red eyes and glistening fangs. Grant nodded in approval.

He went to the window, to the thing that was not quite Pluto. The cat looked up at him and meowed. It must have felt safe with the glass between them.

Grant raked the window with the blade, scratching a thin line across the cat's throat. "You want to play?" said the boy. "You don't play nice."

He looked down at his scraped elbows, suddenly feeling their sting. He figured the pain must have been there all along, somewhere in the back of his mind, slightly out of reach. In fact, he kind of enjoyed the feeling, was enchanted by the sight of his own blood. It wasn't something he saw often.

Outside, behind the cat, heavy wind tore through a row of unruly juniper bushes. Powerful gusts swayed the boughs of a nearby tree that had housed a family of friendly squirrels (and shaded Grant's bedroom) during the previous summer.

"When I open this window," Grant told the cat, "you come right inside."

Pluto 2.0 meowed again and put another paw against the glass. As Grant reached for the latch, the whistling wind decided to roar instead.

With a thunderous crack, one of the tree's branches broke away from its ancient body. The cat leapt away just as the oak's long wooden arm lanced through Grant's bedroom window like a twisted spear.

The boy had the reflexes to sidestep the branch, although he could not dodge shards of glass that flew his way. He felt their wasp stings against his arms and face.

The tree branch had impaled the pigeon's cage, splitting it open down the middle like a walnut shell. Andre fluttered through the newfound gap in the metal and danced along the branch on a single foot before taking flight through the gaping window.

Grant looked down and cursed when he saw that he had knocked over the terrarium with his foot. The spider was on its back, legs kicking in the air. The gecko had crawled to a safer spot, far away from Petey.

Grant did his best to avoid more glass fragments as he leaned through the window and peered outside.

The cat was gone. Grant didn't quite understand how the little devil had known to draw him over to the window, but the boy did know one thing for certain: the black cat had nearly gotten him killed again.

Grant slipped the knife into his pocket and was already planning what to do the next time he saw the cat, when his dad flung open the bedroom door in an epic, red-faced rage.

⊗　⊗　⊗

The next morning, Grant, a groggy zombie, shambled through the hallways of Poe Middle School. Dad had screamed at him for most of the night. Thrown things at him, too, even connecting a couple of times.

That's what happens when your father tries to straighten up your wrecked room and finds an animal graveyard under your bed.

Dad had tossed Grant's collection of bones into the dumpster in the alley out back. Which Grant found sort of funny, because it was the same place the boy had disposed of a black cat in a garbage bag two weeks prior.

Dad had also thrown out a butcher's knife Grant claimed to have used as his killing tool, all the while calling his son nasty things. He had said the boy was sick in the head. Grant didn't disagree.

However, Grant had wholeheartedly disagreed with being driven out to the woods in the middle of the night. He had pleaded with his father, please, please, *please,* not to force him to release his tarantula and gecko into the darkness. His cries went unheard.

Through a veil of tears, the boy had watched Petey and Gordy scramble off into the shadowy brush to fates unknown. He lay awake imagining the worst until the sun rose, when he was pulled off the couch and ordered to go to school.

The boy knew he was closer than ever before to going after his father with the switchblade.

Now Grant turned the corner in front of the school library and saw some other kid, a sixth-grader maybe, standing in front of his locker. It seemed like the scrub was inspecting its door and trying to get a look inside.

"Hey!" Grant shouted, suddenly full of life. "Get away from there!"

He bolted to the kid and shoved him aside.

"What's your problem?" growled the little twerp, rubbing his shoulder. This guy wasn't afraid of Grant at all. "What happened to your face, man?"

Grant had nearly forgotten about the bandages covering his wounds. Surely, they made him look vulnerable. Weak.

"What's *your* problem?" barked Grant. "What are you even *doing* here?"

"This is a free country. I heard something in one of these lockers. Look, in there."

The kid moved for Locker A256, *Grant's* locker.

Grant pushed him again. This time the kid did fall, but he was up in a second flat, rushing the older boy, taking a swing at the seventh-grader.

The kid's fist connected with Grant's jaw. *He hit me*, thought Grant. *He's got to pay.*

Grant, on automatic, without hesitation, pulled the knife from his backpack and flipped the blade open in front of the gutsy brat. The sixth-grader's face went ghost-white.

"You want to mess with me?" Grant asked, gripping the kid's shirt collar, pulling him in close. "Really?"

"No, no, man!" The wide-eyed kid trembled. "Let me go! Please! I'm sorry!"

"You'd better be."

Grant released the smaller boy, who rocketed past him, around the corner, and out of view. Grant smirked.

That's right. Run, wimp. Run for your life.

The bully went to "his" locker and opened it with ease. His two textbooks rested soundlessly inside. Other than that, there was nothing to see. Nothing at all.

Heavy footsteps approached. The click of high heels echoed off the ceiling. An adult was near.

Grant grabbed his textbooks and replaced them with the knife. He quickly yet carefully shut the locker door.

One of the school guidance counselors, Mrs. Sachs, rounded the corner. Next to her was a large man in a bright yellow jacket. Mr. Jones, a security guard. With them was the boy Grant had threatened. Correction: the *snitch* Grant had threatened with the switchblade.

"That's him," the kid said, pointing at his attacker.

"Should've known," growled Mr. Jones.

Mrs. Sachs said to the younger boy, "Stay put, Luis!" She and Mr. Jones walked to Grant, stopping a couple of feet away. The woman had a walkie-talkie in her hand, ready to call for back-up. These people had dealt with Grant before.

"You know why we're here," said the counselor.

Grant stayed silent. In this kind of situation, his tongue was always a gun aiming for his own foot.

Mrs. Sachs sighed. "We're going to have to search you."

Grant opened his arms, inviting them to do their worst. The woman nodded to Mr. Jones, who reached into a pocket and removed a pair of latex gloves. He snapped them over his sausage fingers.

"All right," said the man. "Do you have anything in your pockets that can stick or cut me? Anything in your backpack?"

"No." Grant grinned at the boy standing behind Mrs. Sachs.

Mr. Jones spoke to the counselor. "You heard him."

The security guard patted down Grant's chest, under his arms, along the length of his jeans. Grant rolled his eyes. Did these people really think he was stupid enough to get caught?

"He's clean," said the man.

"Now, the backpack," replied the counselor.

"Right." Mr. Jones held out a hand.

Grant gave the man his bag. The security guard unzipped it, took out a folder, crumpled papers, pens, pencils.

No knife, though.

"There's nothing here," said Mr. Jones.

Grant was ecstatic. "Told you!"

The guard scowled. "You didn't tell me anything."

"He had it!" screeched the sixth-grader. "I swear!"

"Shut up!" Grant felt like choking the little squirt.

"Grant!" Mrs. Sachs silenced him with his name.

Mr. Jones shrugged. "He could've stashed it somewhere."

"Okay," said the counselor. "But where?"

The adults looked along the hallway but found only used tissues and empty bags of chips.

Grant was relieved. It looked like he would get away with another crime. When it came to the nefarious arts, he was quite gifted.

A cat meowed. Grant's blood became liquid nitrogen in his veins.

Mrs. Sachs turned to the sudden noise. "What was that?"

"I don't know," said Mr. Jones.

"I don't hear anything," Grant offered.

Inside Locker A256, a cat meowed louder, louder still.

Grant's heart dropped. How was that even *possible*?

"It's in there!" said the other boy, jabbing a finger in the right direction.

"No," said Grant. He stepped in front of the locker. "No one even uses these things."

Mrs. Sachs said, "Let's check anyway. Mr. Jones?"

The guard told Grant to step aside, but the boy was an immovable boulder. The man said, "Obviously, kid, you're trying to hide something. We'll get inside one way or the other. Just move already."

Grant refused to budge. No way was he giving up so easily.

Locker A256 creaked open on its own.

All eyes saw a black cat sitting beside a gleaming switchblade.

This was it for Grant. Game over.

Pluto 2.0 looked out at Grant and seemed to laugh as the security guard removed the knife. Grant glared.

What *was* the cat? It couldn't be a real animal. A ghost, maybe? A demon? Why was it trying so hard to ruin his life?

It didn't matter. Whatever it was, it had to die.

Grant threw his textbooks to the floor and lunged forward, pushing Mr. Jones aside. The boy wrapped his palms around the cat's throat, squeezing with all of his strength.

The monster was unfazed. It laughed louder, louder still. Its single eye burned with a crimson fire. It slashed at Grant's arms, and the boy felt immense pain. But he let it wash over him. He dived into the agony, headfirst.

The cat then began to grow larger, larger still. It stepped out of the locker, pushing its attacker back. Behind him, Grant faintly heard people shouting, screaming. But he never turned from the changing beast, never lost his focus.

Grant's hands ached as he struggled to strangle the nightmare, but the thing was almost the size of a panther now, its neck as thick as a tree trunk. Its claws and fangs dwarfed the switchblade. The creature no longer laughed. It roared.

The black cat reached up to Grant with muscular limbs, grabbed him by the throat, and lifted him from the ground. Grant finally lost his grip on the fiendish feline and tried kicking the animal instead.

Somehow, the cat hopped back into the locker, dragging Grant along with it. Beast and boy squeezed inside.

Grant wailed as he was dragged deeper inside the locker, deeper still. He was swallowed by darkness, at last realizing that the locker wasn't really a locker at all.

It was a door, and it had opened just for him.

Outside, the door slammed shut and locked tight.

Forever.

A PERFECT CIRCLE

KAILA WAS LOST. As if she needed another reason to think the world was out to get her!

The labyrinthine hallways of Poe Middle School seemed to somehow lead to nowhere and to everywhere at the same time. She would have cried if she thought she could, but she'd cried so much the past few weeks that she was convinced her tear ducts had dried up.

Plus, the last thing she needed as "the new girl" was a reputation for being a crybaby.

Students talked and laughed all around her, not a single one of them reciprocating the weak smile she threw their way. She wondered how long it would take her to get a new group of friends. Then, when she realized her tear ducts worked after all, she forced herself to stop wondering.

As she brushed away all evidence of her frustrations, a tall boy with dark hair and glasses locked eyes with her. He frowned as he walked past, then turned and asked, "Hey, are you okay?"

Kaila said, "Oh . . . um . . . Yeah."

"Really?" He pointed to the class schedule clutched in her trembling hand. "Are you new here?"

"Yes, and, actually, I don't know where I'm going right now. I mean, I know where I'm supposed to be. I just don't know how to get there."

"Can I see that?"

Kaila handed him her schedule.

"Well," said the boy, "at least you get your toughest class out of the way first period." He gave the schedule back. "Follow me. We're going to the same place."

"That's lucky." Kaila smiled in relief.

"You'd think so, but, like I said, Ms. Helda's tough." He offered his hand. "I'm Xavier, by the way."

Kaila shook his hand. "Kaila."

"Nice to meet you." Xavier looked at his watch. "We don't want to be late. Come on."

Kaila followed a step behind Xavier while he parted the sea of students. He walked very fast. He really, really didn't want to be tardy.

"Thanks for helping me out," said Kaila, trying to keep up.

"I try to do at least one good deed a day," Xavier replied.

"I'm not even supposed to be taking Geometry," she said. "I was barely getting a 'C' in Algebra at my last school. Whoever made my schedule made a mistake."

"Good luck trying to convince Ms. Helda of that."

"She's pretty mean, then?"

"Strict. Very strict." Xavier suddenly came to a stop and turned to look Kaila in the eye. "The class is right around this corner. Follow her instructions, don't talk out of turn, and you should be fine."

He led them around a corner and into the back of a very straight, very silent single-file line of students. Outside the other classrooms, kids gossiped and horse-played, but the students in front of Room 113 were focused with almost military-like precision.

The door to 113 slowly creaked open. Ms. Helda appeared. The teacher towered over her students, even though her back was hunched. She had stringy, black hair that fell past her waist and a long, pointy nose with a massive wart resting atop the left nostril.

"Good morning, class," she said. "Your warm-up is on the board."

As the students entered the classroom, Ms. Helda greeted each child with a mischievous grin. Her gray eyes seemed to shine in the fluorescent lights of the hallway.

Kaila was last in line. After Xavier quietly entered the classroom, the Geometry teacher put out a hand that resembled a gigantic spider. "Who might you be, young lady?"

"K-Kaila Michaels." She handed her schedule to Ms. Helda. "They put me in your class even though I was only taking Algebra at my last school."

"Is that so?" The teacher glanced over the schedule and handed it back to Kaila. "There is an empty seat behind Xavier. Since you've already made his acquaintance, perhaps you'd like to sit there for today?"

How did she know Kaila had been talking with Xavier? That was pretty wei—

"You may enter," said the teacher. "Now."

Kaila hurried into the classroom. She immediately realized why all the other kids had been wearing sweatshirts. Room 113 was about as warm as a freezer.

She saw Xavier in the leftmost row of desks. Kaila made her way past a few students furiously working on the warm-up problem and slid into the seat behind him.

"She said I could sit here," Kaila said, but the boy didn't even acknowledge her.

She looked all around. Not a single person seemed to notice "the new girl." Was that good or bad?

Kaila had never seen a classroom as neat as 113. It was impossibly clean. There was not a scrap of paper on the floor, not a hint of graffiti on any desk.

But the problem on the board at the front of the room was just that: a problem. Kaila had no idea what she was looking at.

The Geometry might as well have been written in Mandarin.

"Xavier?" Kaila whispered. "What's a radius?"

There was no answer from her new acquaintance.

"Hey, Xavier. Could you help me out with this?"

Still no answer.

"I told you, I only took Algebra at my old—"

"Excuse me, young lady," said Ms. Helda, who was suddenly standing over Kaila. "We do not speak during the warm-up. Is that understood?"

"I was just asking for some hel—"

"I will not tolerate insolence," Ms. Helda snapped. "Do not talk back to me. You're the student. I'm the teacher." She smiled at Kaila. "Congratulations, you've already earned detention with me."

"But I didn't—"

"Report back here during the break after second period." As she walked away, Ms. Helda said, "You'd better hope this detention with me is your last."

During the rest of Geometry, and even throughout second period History with Mr. Moore, Kaila thought about ditching detention with Ms. Helda. The Geometry teacher was being really unfair. Kaila was new. How was she supposed to know she couldn't speak during class?

On the other hand, Xavier had tried to explain about Ms. Helda, hadn't he? But that wasn't the point. The point was—

"Ah, forget it," Kaila mumbled to herself near the end of second period. She violently scribbled over an unflattering doodle of Ms. Helda in her notebook margin.

She had to go, plain and simple. Her mom was still stressed about the sudden move, and the last thing Kaila wanted was for her mother to get a phone call from the school. That would only make the yelling worse.

The bell rang. Mr. Moore dismissed the students. Kaila quickly packed her things and trudged out of the classroom.

Then it occurred to her that she could pretend she got lost on the way to detention. History class wasn't exactly next door to Geometry. Ms. Helda might understand that.

Kaila snorted. Yeah, right. Ms. Helda didn't seem very understanding.

Once more, chatty, smiling students passed by Kaila in the hallways. Just as before, Kaila walked alone, confused and bitter.

When she rounded the corner to Ms. Helda's classroom, she hoped to see the door shut. Maybe Ms. Helda had forgotten about the detention. Maybe the teacher had gone to refill the coffee mug she had been sipping on during first period.

No such luck. The door was wide open.

Kaila took a couple of deep breaths and walked through the doorway. Ms. Helda stood at the front of the room holding a stack of paper.

"Right on time," said the teacher. "Go to your seat and take out your notebook. The one you like to draw in."

How did she know about the noteb—?

"Now, young lady. Let's not dawdle."

Kaila bolted to her seat. From her backpack, she produced the notebook and placed it on the desk.

Ms. Helda was suddenly beside her. Like a gnarled claw, the teacher's hand unfurled in front of Kaila's face. Lying in the middle of Ms. Helda's palm was a pencil.

At least Kaila thought it was a pencil. It seemed to be crafted out of some kind of dark, scarred wood. There was a point at one end but no eraser at the other.

"Take it," Ms. Helda ordered.

Kaila shivered and took the odd-looking pencil from the teacher. It was almost as heavy as a roll of pennies.

The teacher said, "Draw a perfect circle with this, and it will end." She turned away from Kaila and walked toward the door. "I need to run off some copies in the teachers' lounge."

Before Kaila could say a word, Ms. Helda had slammed the door shut behind her. There was a loud click, and then . . . silence.

Kaila jumped up. Wait! Did the teacher just—?

She ran to the door and twisted the knob. It didn't budge. She was locked in!

Was that even allowed? For a second, she forgot the plan was to not mention the detention. Wait until she told her mom about—No. She couldn't do that.

Kaila jiggled the knob a few more times and then gave up. "You've got to be kidding me!" she shouted to the ceiling. She threw up her arms and again noticed the strange weight of the pencil in her hand.

Finally, she flopped back down into her seat and flipped the notebook open to a blank page. All she had to do was draw a circle? It was a weird request, but at least it was an easy one.

She pressed the pencil's point to the page. A shape appeared on the paper, but it wasn't a circle. It was an oval, maybe. Kaila could certainly do better than that.

She drew again. This time, the "circle" was fat at its bottom and narrow at its top. She had drawn an egg. This wasn't going as well as she had hoped.

As she was about to try again, the shapes in the notebook began to glow. A deep red light burned around their edges like a lit cannon fuse.

Kaila leaned closer to the notebook. Was she seeing things?

The middle of each shape swirled with darkness. It was as if some unseen artist had filled them in with an invisible paintbrush.

"What the—?" Kaila whispered.

Within seconds, she was looking at two dark holes on her paper. A faint, warm breeze drifted from within the holes and kissed her forehead.

Kaila brought her face even closer to the page. The holes didn't seem to have a bottom: just darkness, and it went on forever.

She pulled a gum wrapper from her pants pocket, balled it up and dropped it into one of the holes. The silver wrapper disappeared as it was swallowed up by the darkness.

Kaila tore the paper from the notebook and looked at the back of it. The holes didn't go through the page. They somehow remained on only one side of the paper.

She threw the pencil to the ground. What had she done? She had drawn—*opened*—holes to . . . where? Another world?

Opening portals to other dimensions! Yeah, right! That was stupid!

Wasn't it?

Kaila dropped the page to the desk. She stood and backed away, shaking her head in disbelief.

Growls erupted from the abyss of each hole. Something was on the other side, after all.

Then, dozens of long, squid-like tentacles exploded from the darkness of each hole and wrapped around Kaila's wrists. She shrieked as she was pulled toward the paper.

Kaila tried to hold her ground, but whatever monster was on the other side was strong. Too strong. Larger, slimier tentacles pushed the holes open wider. They reached for Kaila's throat. Her cries drowned beneath the thunderous roars.

Kaila's sneakers screeched against the tile floor. She was in the middle of a tug-of-war for her life.

The tentacles seeped translucent goop. The slime was sticky and held to Kaila's flesh like glue. It also stank worse than a wet diaper pile, and Kaila nearly puked.

Instead, she focused on yanking her arms back with all her might. "Let. Go. Of. Me." All her muscles were on fire.

She seemed to only be moving closer to the widening holes. They were horrible mouths ready to bite off her head.

"No!" she screamed. "NO!"

Veins throbbed in her neck. She pulled back harder than she had ever thought possible.

Tentacles tore as Kaila ripped free of the beast. The momentum sent the girl sprawling backward to the floor.

The monster bellowed. Purple goo sprayed from its tentacle stumps. It was in pain. Enraged.

Kaila rubbed her arms, getting some leftover tentacle snot on her fingers. Her arms were covered in welts from the tentacles' collection of suckers. She was lucky that they hadn't torn off patches of her skin.

Kaila somehow found the strength to get back on her feet. More tentacles swiped at her ankles and calves, but she dodged them and made it to the door.

She rattled the doorknob. It was still locked. She pounded the door with her fists. Rivers streamed down her cheeks. She screamed for help, choking on tears.

Couldn't anyone hear the madness going on inside Room 113?

Kaila turned to see tentacles still approaching, hundreds of them: different sizes, different colors. They seemed to fill the room as they slithered around, toppling desks and chairs.

The unholy holes had completely devoured the paper from where they originated, and now they hung in the air like rifts in the very fabric of reality.

When Kaila had first drawn them, the misshapen "circles" were no bigger than a pizza-cutter blade. Now, the creature from the other side had pushed them open to the size of sewer covers.

Ferocious gusts of wind poured from these "rifts," as well. Kaila felt as if she was in the middle of a tornado as the forceful flurries sent papers twirling off Ms. Helda's desk.

The tentacles were almost upon her.

There was nothing she could do. She was going to die. The creature would pull her through the rifts and consume her slowly with razor-sharp fangs.

This was it. Her life was over.

Kaila squeezed her eyes shut and accepted her fate. She would never see her mom again. There would be no more laughter, no more friends.

That's when Ms. Helda's words flooded back into her mind: *"Draw a perfect circle with this, and it will end."*

Kaila's eyes opened wide.

It will end.

She had to get that pencil back.

Within seconds, Kaila had hurdled the tentacles and was back where she had thrown the pencil. She was dangerously close to the ever-widening rifts, with more and more tentacles swarming around her.

But she couldn't find the pencil. Panicking, she imagined that the creature had pulled it through to the other side.

Then she spotted it on the floor, a few inches from her left foot. As Kaila reached for the pencil, a powerful tentacle wrapped around her waist. It squeezed with anaconda strength and lifted her from the ground.

"No!" Kaila wheezed.

Good thing she had been able to wrap her fingers around the pencil before the tentacle struck. *It will end.*

Kaila stabbed the tentacle with the pencil. Rancid ooze spurted from the wounds, and the beast screeched, releasing its hold on her.

She landed on her feet and raced to the front of the room, dodging other strikes. The wind was now powerful enough to almost knock her to the ground.

An object rolled off Ms. Helda's desk and thudded to the floor. The wind slid the teacher's empty coffee mug toward Kaila.

"Draw a perfect circle, and it will end."

Draw a circle. Draw a circle.

No, draw a *perfect* circle.

It will end.

Drawing the circles free-hand had resulted in the current horror. She needed something round. Something she could trace.

A perfect circle.

The coffee mug bumped against Kaila's right shoe. The bottom of the mug was round, shaped by an expert's mold or by a machine. Surely, it was a perfect circle. Or close enough. It was worth a shot.

Kaila grabbed the mug, then darted to Ms. Helda's desk and ducked behind it. The massive piece of furniture blocked some of the wind.

She snatched a piece of flying paper from the air. On the floor, she steadied the mug's bottom against the page as well as she could.

Beast and wind screamed. Beside Kaila, the desk shifted. Whether from monstrous tentacles or powerful gust, Kaila did not know. Quite frankly, she didn't care. She was too focused on keeping the mug still.

"*Draw a perfect circle, and it will end.*"

Kaila held the mug with her left hand and the pencil with her right. She hesitated. What if she drew another imperfect circle and it created a different hole in reality? There was no way she would survive that.

Two tentacles snaked over and around the desk.

"No way." Kaila quickly, but carefully, traced the pencil around the mug's round edges.

She lifted the mug to see her circle on the page. It looked perfect. It had to be.

Tentacles crept up her right pants leg and wrapped around her knee. Kaila yelped. She stabbed with the pencil again.

The tentacles! There were too many of them! They were there! Right there!

She was toast.

The new, perfect circle glowed with a golden light. The tentacles came closer. The creature snarled louder. The wind howled like a hurricane.

The perfect circle glowed brighter, brighter. It was so beautiful. Kaila smiled. She actually laughed.

"*Draw a perfect circle, and it will end.*"

The golden light from the page was too much for Kaila to bear. She closed her eyes and covered them with her hands.

And, then, it ended.

The growls and howls were no more.

Kaila moved her hands and opened her eyes. The room was in pristine condition and completely still. There were no rifts, no tentacles, no wind. The drawing of the perfect circle was also gone. It was as if nothing had ever happened.

The door creaked open. Ms. Helda stood in the doorway.

"Get out from behind my desk," snapped the teacher.

Kaila stood on shaky legs and practically ran to Ms. Helda. "Glad to see you," she said in a trembling voice.

"Really, now?" The teacher held out a small slip of paper to Kaila. "It seems that an error was made. You aren't supposed to be enrolled in my class, after all."

Kaila looked up into Ms. Helda's glowing gray eyes. "Are you serious?"

"I am always serious," said Ms. Helda. "It looks like you won't be serving detention in this classroom ever again."

"Thank goodness!" Kaila practically jumped with delight.

She darted over to her backpack and notebook and snatched them up in her arms. Ms. Helda approached.

Kaila held the pencil out to the teacher and said, "No offense, but I don't ever want to come back."

Ms. Helda took the pencil. "Is that so?"

Once through the doorway, Kaila saw a familiar face.

"Xavier!" she cried.

The boy turned. "Hey. Kaila, right?"

"Yeah."

"You survived detention. Welcome to the club."

Kaila nervously smiled. "Can you show me where my actual math class is?" She handed him the paper Ms. Helda had given her.

Xavier nodded. "Mr. Ford, huh? Not quite as bad as Ms. Helda, but you should still follow some guidelines. You'll listen this time, right?"

She grinned. "I will. Thanks." Was she making a friend already?

Kaila hurried down the hall with Xavier, staying in step with the boy's long legs, not once looking back at Room 113.

DANCES WITH WOLF

WHEN SABRINA HAD SOLD Spring Fling tickets at lunch, she noticed that Ruben Gutierrez had waited a few extra minutes to buy his ticket specifically from her. "You'll be at the dance, right?" he asked.

"Of course," Sabrina said, a stupid grin on her face. She wondered if he heard the nervous crack in her voice.

"Cool." Ruben handed her the money for his ticket. "I'll definitely see you there."

"Yes, you will."

Once Sabrina handed him his ticket, Ruben turned and rejoined his friends. He hadn't asked her to be his date like she had prayed he would, but Sabrina was satisfied enough with the moments they had shared.

Every night, Sabrina practiced slow-dancing in her bedroom. She would clutch a large pillow in her arms, pretend it was Ruben, and slowly turn in circles in front of her full-length mirror. She imagined what he would say into her ear over whatever love song played. She knew exactly how she would giggle if he told a joke.

The Spring Fling was going to be perfect . . . until it wasn't.

◉　◉　◉

The Monday before the big night, there was a knock at Sabrina's bedroom door. She was updating her Faboo page when she should have been doing homework.

Sabrina quickly minimized the window on her laptop, picked up a pencil, and shouted at the door, "Yeah?"

"Honey, *abuela* is here with your dress," her dad said from the other side.

It was about time! Sabrina had been waiting weeks for her grandmother to alter her cousin's old *quinceanera* ensemble.

"I want you to try it on with me here," said *abuela*.

"Okay! Come in!" Sabrina said, perhaps a little too excited.

The door swung open. Her dad took a step inside, looking at her suspiciously. "How's the homework going?"

"Fine," Sabrina smiled. "I'm ready for a break."

Sabrina's grandmother entered the room. "Glad I could make it, then." The woman clutched a hanger that held a gorgeous blue dress. "*Hola, mija.*"

"Hi!" Sabrina hopped out of her seat and practically ran into her grandmother's warm hug.

"She's never that excited to see me," said her father.

Sabrina hugged him tightly, as well. "I'll leave you two alone, I guess," he said. "Come model this dress in the living room when you're ready."

The old woman looked up at her son. "You think I'd make her a dress that made her look like some naughty girl?"

"Not at all, Ma." Sabrina's dad kissed *abuela* on the forehead. "I just want to see how beautiful she looks."

The man then turned and left the two ladies alone in the room. Sabrina's grandmother laid the dress out on the bed.

Sabrina beamed. "It looks great."

"Oh, I know," said *abuela*. "Your mom kept calling me, asking me when it would be ready. I said, 'What's the rush?' She said you just wanted it early, so here it is."

"Early?" said Sabrina. "The dance is Friday."

"Next Friday, your mom said."

"This Friday, *abuela*."

"This Friday?" The old woman was puzzled. "No, next Friday."

"No, it's this week. That's why I wanted the dress."

"Sabrina," *abuela* said, serious and concerned. "Your parents think the dance is next week."

"It's okay. They'll still let me go. My grades are better now. I just passed my Health test. And I'm not getting in trouble anymore at school."

"You can't go this Friday, *mija*."

Butterflies bustled inside Sabrina's stomach. And they were getting angry.

"Why?" said Sabrina. "What's the difference?"

"*La luna llena*," said the old woman. "It's this Friday night."

Sabrina's heart sank like a stone. She raced over to the computer and Googled what *abuela* had just told her.

Sabrina read the information displayed on the laptop's screen. Her grandmother was right. How could Sabrina have been so clueless?

"No . . ." She collapsed into her chair and began to cry. Her heart now sank like a boulder.

La luna llena.

The full moon.

A werewolf's worst nightmare.

After a long family meeting, Sabrina's parents decided she could still attend the dance on Friday. They just wanted to remind her of the risks.

Only full-blooded werewolves were dangerous. That's why *abuela* and Sabrina's father had to sometimes be locked in steel cages when *la luna llena* was in the sky.

Sabrina was not a full-blooded werewolf. Her mother was a normal human being. Therefore, Sabrina was only a half-breed. When half-breeds transformed, they grew fur, became super strong, and looked ferocious, but they had the minds and behaviors of a regular person.

As a werewolf, Sabrina merely looked like a monster. She rarely ever actually acted like one.

Still, her parents warned her that if the light of the full moon hit her skin while she was at the dance, she would most certainly transform. In front of the entire school.

Sabrina had to realize that going outside at all during the full moon was a huge risk. Family tradition was to close the blinds, drapes, and shutters on *la luna llena*. Nights of the full moon were almost always movie marathon events, complete with popcorn and candy.

On occasion, slivers of moonlight escaped the covered windows. The cages in the basement were for whenever *abuela* or Dad got out of hand.

If Sabrina ever accidentally transformed, her mom would brush her fur and scratch her behind the ears. It was nice, sure, but Sabrina always tried her best to avoid transformation if she could. Changing into a wolf was an uncomfortable, bone-wrenching process.

The timing of the Spring Fling couldn't have been worse, but Sabrina just had to go. It might be the only evening formal dance the school would ever have. If standardized test scores dropped, Sabrina doubted students would be rewarded with another event as cool as this one.

Plus, only total losers were going to miss it. And Ruben would probably find another girl if Sabrina didn't show. She absolutely couldn't let that happen.

So Sabrina decided to risk humiliation. She would wear the gorgeous blue dress (which fit perfectly, by the way). Outside, she would do her best to hide from moonlight while wearing a big hooded sweatshirt. She would also stay in the shadows.

Sabrina was fairly confident the full moon wouldn't be a problem.

⊚   ⊚   ⊚

Friday night, Sabrina made sure to arrive at the middle school before sunset. As a member of the student council, she had to help take care of any last-minute preparations in the gymnasium, anyway.

She checked her hoodie at the door with one of the teacher chaperones. She then entered the gymnasium to help string up decorations.

Her werewolf senses were on overdrive. The collective odor of two hundred latex-rubber balloons assaulted her nostrils like an intense tidal wave. Sabrina could also smell every part of the hot pizza pies stacked in the corner of the room. The baked dough, the marinara sauce, the melted mozzarella cheese, the pepperoni, the mushrooms, the green bell peppers, the black olives . . .

Sabrina heard paper crinkle as streamers unfurled and fell to the floor. High heels clacked against the hardwood floor, echoing in her ears.

Sabrina was surprised to find Ruben helping to secure things to the walls. He wasn't even on the student council. What was he doing there so early? Had he come just for the pizza?

Sabrina approached the boy. "Hey, Ruben."

"Hey." He smiled. He wore some kind of cologne. It sort of smelled like deer musk. But Sabrina wasn't going to tell him that. At least he was making an effort.

"You're early," she said to him.

"I know," he said. "I was just excited. I guess I couldn't wait."

Why was he so excited? Was it to see Sabrina?

"You look very pretty," Ruben added. She sensed nervousness in his voice.

"Thanks," Sabrina replied.

She knew how good she looked. Her mom had helped her with her hair and make-up. A white corsage rested on her left wrist. It smelled fresher than the ones other girls wore around the room.

"You look very nice, too." Sabrina's cheeks became hot.

Ruben's baby blue collared shirt matched her dress and his

eyes. He also wore a pink tie, which Sabrina thought was great. Only the best, most confident guys wore pink.

Ruben laughed and thanked her for the compliment. "Help me with the balloons, okay?"

She got closer to him. His scent was growing on her by the second.

For the next forty-five minutes Sabrina's world consisted of her interactions with Ruben. They told stories, and whenever Ruben said something funny, Sabrina had the perfect giggle. Twice, while they secured balloons to the walls, their hands touched. Sabrina was never the first to pull away.

Then the dance began. The lights dimmed. The D.J. spun his records. The music was too loud for Sabrina's taste, but she didn't complain. Ruben seemed to be enjoying the tunes. He bobbed his head up and down to the rhythm.

The punch bowl splashed. The photo booth flashed.

Within minutes, it seemed like the entire school had arrived. Sabrina was jumping up and down inside.

She noticed that some moonlight had crept in through the front doors, so she didn't venture too far from where the D.J. was staged.

She and Ruben talked and laughed, laughed and talked. Ruben seemed to think he had to yell in order for Sabrina to hear him over the music and screaming kids, but Sabrina's werewolf ears could hear him just fine.

The two of them didn't dance. Yet. The music was really upbeat and they both seemed cautious about showing off their skills . . . if they had any at all.

Eventually, some of Ruben's friends found him with Sabrina. They tried to pull him away from her, but he told them he wanted to stay. Ruben's friends begrudgingly stayed by his side. Which was fine, except that the boys had applied far too much body spray to themselves.

Some of Sabrina's friends showed up next to her on the dance floor. Their flowery perfumes fought off the pungent cloud of body spray. The boys eventually found the courage to flirt with the girls. Soon enough, they were one large group, singing, laughing, and dancing together. The entire time, Ruben stayed by Sabrina's side.

She was in heaven, even though she began to smell her own salty sweat over Ruben's comforting scent.

Of course, that's when a couple of immature sixth-graders decided it would be a good idea to try to sneak out of the gymnasium through a side door.

A wedge of moonlight entered through the open doorway and hit Sabrina on the shoulder.

Almost immediately, a wave of nausea hit her.

Sabrina took a step back from the group and looked down at her hands. Dark fur was sprouting on her knuckles like lightning-quick weeds.

"Sabrina?" Ruben said. "Are you okay?"

Sabrina didn't dare open her mouth. She grimaced. Her teeth were already growing into fangs.

She ran.

Sabrina plowed through the side door. Mr. West no longer stood guard, since he was running after those pesky sixth-grade jerks.

She was now completely awash in moonlight. *La luna llena* seemed to taunt her from above.

Sabrina would have cried, if her tear ducts hadn't disappeared.

Sabrina raced across the blacktop. Where was she going? There was nowhere to hide. Most of the school was locked, and she didn't dare go toward the front where other students could see her.

She stumbled a couple of times in her heels until her feet turned into enormous paws and tore the shoes apart. The dress stretched and the corsage snapped as her bones and muscles expanded.

She screamed in pain and frustration, and what came out

instead was a loud, wounded howl.

Her sensitive wolf ears picked up shouts and footfalls behind her. Someone was following her.

She didn't dare look back. She had to get out of there.

She was now on all-fours, quickly loping toward the P.E. field. She would hop the fence and figure out what to do next.

"Sabrina!" a hoarse voice growled. "Wait!"

But she didn't wait. She ran faster and faster, no longer a girl, now a bullet-like creature of the night.

Impossibly, whoever was behind her seemed to be gaining ground. Sabrina stopped at the edge of the P.E. field when she heard a pained howl.

Twenty feet away, another wolf watched her, his head held low to the ground. He looked at her with amazing blue eyes. A tattered, pink tie dangled around his throat. He sort of smelled like deer musk.

Ruben whimpered. "Sabrina, will you please stop running away from me?"

"Ruben, you're . . . You're . . ."

"Just like you," he said as sweetly as he could with his were-wolf growl. "See?"

Sabrina shook her head. "But . . . but . . ."

He approached her. "I think it's great."

Sabrina held her ground. "You do?"

"Yeah," he said. "You look even prettier than before."

That's when Sabrina discovered werewolves could also blush. She said, "You look really cute, too."

"I wasn't sure about you. Not until tonight." He nuzzled up against her. He was so soft. Softer than any pillow.

"Is that right?" She giggled.

"Tonight, you've changed a lot in my eyes."

"Oh, yeah?"

"I thought I smelled something a bit . . . familiar on you. Good thing I trusted my instincts."

Sabrina said, "I guess I should've been sniffing even more

around you, too, huh?"

Ruben laughed. "But then maybe tonight's surprise would've been ruined."

"You're probably right."

Even though they were now on the other side of the campus, both of their ears perked up at the sound of a slow love song playing in the gymnasium.

"Can I have this dance?" Ruben asked.

"Yes. Since you asked so nicely."

Sabrina looked up at *la luna llena* and grinned, revealing bright fangs. The two wolves embraced under the light of the full moon and moved along with the far-off melody.

Then, an aluminum can loudly rolled across the asphalt behind them, successfully ruining their magical moment.

Both wolves turned to find a short boy in a suit standing a few meters away from them. Mouth agape, he trembled in the dark, near the can he'd accidentally struck with his tennis shoe.

Sabrina recognized the boy as one of the sixth-graders who'd opened the side door to the gymnasium. He must've gotten away from Mr. West somehow, only to now find himself in the presence of dancing monsters.

The kid gulped, waved, and said, "Uh . . . hi . . ."

The wolves broke apart from one another. They shared a worried glance.

Ruben asked Sabrina, "You know him?"

Sabrina shook her head. "Not really."

The boy replied, "I'm . . . I'm Kirk . . ."

Sabrina said to Ruben, "How'd we not smell him? Hear him?"

Ruben answered, "I think something beautiful was distracting me."

Sabrina immediately wanted to nuzzle up against him again. But first . . .

First, they had to take care of little Kirk.

She said, "I don't want people to know about this . . . my

secret."

Ruben shook his head. "Me, neither. My mom's always said, 'If somebody knows you're a werewolf, they'll either try to kill you or they'll get you killed. So, kill them first.'"

Sabrina's family had similar beliefs. That's why they worked so hard to stay out of the spotlight on *la luna llena*. Because accidents could happen, and in order to cover them up, blood had to spill.

The wolves stepped toward Kirk. The sixth-grader took steps away from them.

He said, "I . . . I don't even really know what you look like when you're . . . when you're normal. And . . . And I don't know your names! I swear!"

"Do you believe him?" Ruben said.

Sabrina shrugged. "I'm not sure."

The wolves took another step toward the boy.

"You . . . You don't have to do this!" Kirk pleaded. "Please! Let me go!"

"We can't," Sabrina solemnly said. "Sorry, but it's the only way that we and our families stay safe."

Kirk knew what was coming next. He ran. He was pretty quick, too.

The wolves were quicker.

They caught up to him within seconds. Each beast grabbed an ankle and dragged the boy, shrieking, behind a shadowy dumpster.

Kirk cried out for help until Ruben clamped his jaws down around the boy's throat.

As her adrenaline faded in the aftermath of the kill, Sabrina said, "Now what? I'm not going to eat that."

"Neither am I; that's nasty," said Ruben. "We just leave him here and hope it gets blamed on a coyote." He sniffed the air. "You smell that?"

Sabrina raised her snout and inhaled. She smelled garbage. Spoiled milk, snotty tissue, soggy cardboard . . .

"Well, well, well . . ." said Ruben. Sabrina followed his gaze.

A plump raccoon sat atop the overflowing trashbin. It hissed at the wolves.

"What do you think?" Ruben said. "Are you hungry?"

Sabrina licked her chops. "It depends. Do I have to share?"

Ruben laughed. Sabrina wasn't sure if he was just being polite or if he actually thought what she said was funny. Either way, it was cute.

The raccoon leapt from the dumpster and scurried off.

The wolves chased after it, giggling together and howling into the unforgettable night.

TASTES WEIRD

THE BELL RANG FOR lunch, and students poured out of their classrooms like hordes of starving locusts. Kids ran for the cafeteria so they could be among the first in line for the midday meal.

Steven always found this odd, because no one really cared for the cafeteria cuisine. Yet people pushed and clawed toward the food anyway.

Steven's best friend, Javy, was one of the lemmings who always got a decent spot in line. Javy's fourth period Art class was across campus, so he was never quite at the front. However, Javy was a pretty fast miler, so he often fell within the first fifty students at the cafeteria.

This was good for Steven, because it meant he never had to wait long in the lunch line. Javy always saved him a spot.

On this particular Tuesday, Javy was all smiles when Steven met him at the cafeteria. Javy was practically dancing out of his sneakers.

"Hey." Steven slipped in line behind Javy. "Why are you so happy?"

"Because." Javy giggled. "There's supposed to be some kind of dessert today!"

Steven rolled his eyes. "Okay, but it's *cafeteria* dessert. Why get your hopes up about that?"

"Dessert is dessert."

Steven shook his head. "Not when it's made here."

Javy licked his lips. "I hope it's *flan*."

"I hope it's not," said Steven. "Not because I don't like *flan*, but because I'm afraid what the cafeteria's version of *flan* would taste like."

Javy nodded. "I guess you're right. Most of the food here is . . ."

"Inedible?" Steven offered.

"Gross," Javy agreed.

"Hazardous to our health."

"Nasty."

"Horrible."

Javy grinned. "*Scary*," he said.

Steven laughed.

Two sixth-graders walked out of the cafeteria, past the line-up. Styrofoam lunch trays looked huge in their tiny hands.

"Can you see what they have?" Javy asked. "I can't tell."

"You're taller than I am, Javy."

Other students craned their necks, hoping to catch a glimpse of whatever was on today's menu. Rumors of rubbery chicken fingers and soggy French fries filtered through the line.

"Well," said Steven, "it could be worse."

"Yeah," said Javy. "It could be tuna casserole. Or meatloaf."

"*Raccoon* loaf," Steven corrected.

"You're going to make me sick."

"The cafeteria will do that for you."

A classmate of theirs, Lorna, walked by with her lunch tray. Sitting next to her carton of low-fat milk was a cup of—

"Ice cream!" Javy shouted. In line around them, students murmured excitedly.

Steven's stomach rumbled. They had never served ice cream

at school before. As more students walked by, Steven realized there was some variety to this treat. There were actually different flavors to choose from!

Within minutes, Javy and Steven were at their usual table in the cafeteria. Neither boy had even bothered to sit down before digging into his dessert with a plastic spork.

"How's yours?" said Javy, his mouth full of chocolate ice cream.

"Awesome," was the only word Steven could use to describe the strawberry-flavored treat in front of him.

The dessert was creamier and sweeter than any he had tried before. Each bite was a taste of heaven.

Why hadn't the cafeteria ever served this in the past? Kids could have been indulging themselves for years!

A shrill shriek pierced the crowd. Some girl a few tables over pointed down to her lunch tray. A spork quivered in her grasp.

Like wildfire, word spread that the girl had found a dead spider in her ice cream. Kids pushed aside their trays, appetites suddenly lost. Other students picked at their food, searching for hidden creepy crawlies.

But not Steven and Javy. The boys gobbled up the last of their dessert and then went outside to play soccer with some of the other seventh-grade boys.

On Wednesday, the cafeteria served ice cream again. Steven tried the chocolate, while Javy went for vanilla. On Thursday, ice cream was served again. This time, Javy went back to chocolate and Steven had vanilla. On Friday, Steven and Javy both scarfed down some strawberry.

Each day a student screamed over something strange found in his or her dessert. On Wednesday, an eighth-grade girl discovered a worm curled at the bottom of her cup. On Thursday, a sixth-grade boy bit into a juicy earwig that pinched the tip of his tongue. On Friday, the upper half of a cockroach twitched inside Anthony Becerra's chocolate ice cream.

On Monday, after Apryl Lee found a rat's tail in her strawberry treat, Steven finally asked Javy, "Don't you think it's weird that kids keep finding gross stuff in the ice cream?"

Javy looked down at his own empty cup of chocolate. "Well, I haven't found anything weird in mine."

"Yet." Steven pushed his half-eaten vanilla ice cream aside.

"You done with that?" Javy asked.

"It's all yours."

"Sweet!" Javy took the rest of his friend's dessert. "Thanks, man. I can't get enough of this stuff."

On Tuesday and Wednesday, Steven first noticed the lunch staff. Of course, the workers had always been there, but he had never really paid attention to them until now.

Each time a student made a disgusting dessert discovery, the staff members laughed. They giggled and guffawed. They smiled and smirked.

"They're putting things into the ice cream on purpose," Steven told Javy.

"I don't know." Javy spoke with a mouth full of strawberry. "Why would they do that?"

"They're twisted," said Steven. "I mean, you have to be pretty twisted to work all day inside a sweaty school cafeteria, but these people are *really* twisted."

Javy shrugged. "Maybe they're just bored."

Steven sighed. "I'm never eating that ice cream again. That's guaranteed."

"Good," said Javy. "More for me, then."

Javy was already taking unwanted desserts from various other students. In a week, his mile time had slowed a few seconds and his waistline had gained a couple of pounds.

"Aren't you suspicious?" Steven said.

"Nope," said Javy. "Just hungry."

The next day, hungry, hungry Javy dug into the vanilla ice cream on Steven's tray. He almost chomped down on a seagull's severed, webbed foot.

Javy wailed like a wounded warthog. Steven's ears nearly bled from the noise.

While Javy screeched, Steven noticed the lunch staff nodding in approval. One man actually applauded, while two ladies high-fived behind the sneeze-guard.

Now, why would they do that?

Javy was out of school for the rest of the week. When Steven finally called Javy's home on Saturday, the boy's mother said that her son was sick.

"Will he be at school on Monday?" Steven asked.

"We don't know, dear," said Javy's mother. "Probably not. The doctor is still figuring out what's wrong with him."

"Will he be okay?" said Steven.

"He should be. He's just really tired."

"Well . . . Tell him I hope he feels better soon."

"I will, dear. Thank you for calling."

Steven was left staring at the phone in his hand. Dial tone filled the still air.

Did the ice cream have something to do with Javy's illness?

During Homeroom on Monday, the assistant principal, Mr. Dupin, announced that a "rare strain of flu" was spreading around campus. Many students were falling ill, and the administrator advised students and faculty to keep their hands clean and to get a good night's rest.

Steven struggled to sleep every night that week. Javy had not made it back to school. The boy's mother sounded more and more worried over the phone.

"He's had a fever for days," she said. "He won't eat a thing, and he's getting delirious. He won't stop talking about ice cream, but that's the last thing his body needs right now."

Now, during every lunch, multiple students were finding inappropriate items inside their dessert. The lunch staff always seemed overly pleased by this.

Steven had seen—and heard—enough. It was time to involve the proper authorities.

Steven approached the assistant principal in the hall one

morning before school.

"Mr. Dupin?" he asked a portly, bald man with glasses. "Do you know what's going on in the cafeteria at lunch?"

"Of course I do," said the administrator. "And I'm going to make sure it stops today."

"You are?" Steven beamed. "That's great!"

"I've been hearing lots of complaints lately. Don't worry, young man. I'll make sure you feel safe in the cafeteria from now on."

"Thanks!" Steven walked away, smiling. The cafeteria workers were doomed.

When Steven went into the cafeteria later that day, Mr. Dupin stood guard near the entrance. The lunch staff was going down.

Steven never got ice cream anymore, so he kept his eagle eyes on other students who tempted fate with sporkfuls of the dessert. He found himself wishing that some kid would bite into something gross already, so that the assistant principal could spring into action.

A few minutes later, Steven got his wish. Sort of.

Mr. Dupin locked his gaze onto a couple of boys who were a few tables away from Steven. The man darted across the room toward the kids. Steven hadn't heard a scream. What was going on?

He watched the assistant principal argue with the larger of the two boys. Mr. Dupin made the boy stand from his seat and empty his pockets. The smaller boy nodded and pointed to some crumpled dollar bills.

Wait a second . . . This was what Mr. Dupin meant by keeping the cafeteria "safe"? He was shaking down bullies who picked on other kids for their lunch money?

The bully handed crinkly cash back to his victim. Mr. Dupin then quickly escorted the hulking jerk out of the cafeteria.

Seriously?! The adults around school were never any help! Steven wasn't sure if it was because they were clueless or because they were careless. Either way, they were useless!

A minute later, some girl squealed. A surprise in her ice

cream. Cafeteria workers chuckled.

Steven cracked his knuckles, ready to finally take matters into his own hands. Ready to solve this mystery and scrub the smiles off some lunch staff faces.

That night at home, Steven concocted a plan. He'd sneak into the cafeteria kitchen after school, when the lunch staff thought they were all alone. He'd eavesdrop on whatever disturbing conversations they had with one another. He'd also take video on his phone if he heard or saw anything suspicious and noteworthy.

In the garage, he found a roll of duct tape and a water pistol. The tape was for the bottoms of his shoes. The Internet said that applying duct tape to the bottoms of shoes helps a person to walk around more quietly. Perfect for sneaking around a creepy kitchen.

The water pistol was for self-defense. In the morning, Steven would fill it to the brim with hot sauce from his family's fridge. He wouldn't hesitate to squirt the eyes of any cafeteria worker who got too close to him.

In his bedroom, Steven drew a monster's face onto a piece of paper. He taped it to the wall. A paper target. He filled the plastic pistol with water and practiced his aim.

Shots spattered against the paper face and dripped down the creature's cheeks like tears.

Yeah, tomorrow the hot sauce would definitely get Steven some answers.

As Steven perfected his shots, Javy's mother called. She was distraught.

Javy had gone missing. His bedroom window was wide-open. It seemed like he had run away.

He'd left behind no note, no clues of his whereabouts. Only puddles of melted ice cream in his bed.

"Steven, dear, please tell me you know where he is!" Javy's mother begged. "He's not thinking clearly! Is this all because I wouldn't let him have any dessert?! He snuck some ice cream into his room and then ran off to get more?! Is that what this is?!"

Steven didn't really know what to say. He had no way to give the sobbing woman the comfort that she sought.

Even though he had no answers, Steven knew a few people who might.

He spent the rest of the night firing laser-like streams against the wall.

After school the next day, Steven secured duct tape to the bottoms of his sneakers and went to the cafeteria. The doors were slightly ajar. He creaked one open just wide enough for him to slip through.

Inside, the cafeteria was dark and lifeless. Steven had never been in the room when it was so silent.

Then a familiar sound split the air: the scream of a terrified child.

It came from the kitchen. Steven wiped sweaty palms against his jeans. Was he really going through with this? He was no hero. Was he?

He took a deep breath and lifted the hot sauce pistol from his backpack. He'd spent hours training for this moment. Steven walked forward, a trembling knight in no armor.

He entered the kitchen in a crouch. He peered around a counter and immediately held back a gasp.

Lunch staff members crowded around a table like maniacal nurses in an evil operating room. Strapped to the table was a sobbing girl. She was the same girl who had found a used Band-Aid in her ice cream at lunch earlier in the day.

A monstrous contraption dangled from the ceiling above the girl. It was metallic and spider-like, with a long hose attached to its front, like a twisted elephant's trunk.

"No!" The girl squirmed. "Leave me alone!"

"We know this is frightening," a lunch lady said.

"Really, that's the whole point," said a tall man in a stained apron.

"Just know you're helping us, dear," said a woman with red hair. "You should feel good about that."

The girl spat and shrieked again.

"Be proud," a man with a thick mustache and beard offered. He wore a hairnet over his facial hair. "Your screams are so impressive."

"Why are you *doing* this?" the girl asked, struggling against her restraints.

"Because," Redhead said, "you're going to make us rich."

A different lady snorted. "You're going to make our *dessert* rich. Flavorful."

Before the girl could say anything more, Tall Man secured the machine's dangling hose to a clear plastic facemask and pressed it against the girl's nose and mouth, muffling her cries.

The cafeteria workers put on little facemasks of their own. Ones made of paper to protect themselves from whatever was about to come.

With the flip of a switch, the monstrous machine whirred. The girl's body convulsed. A glowing meter on the side of the machine descended a bit more after each of her stifled shrieks. Steam traveled down the hose and into the girl's mask, into her screaming mouth. Some of it escaped around the edges of the mask and began to fog up the kitchen.

But it wasn't steam . . . Steam wasn't yellow . . .

The lunch staff was pumping the girl full of noxious gas.

This was insane! Steven had his phone out, zooming in on and recording the madness with a shaky hand.

Tall Man kept a close eye on the machine's falling meter. He was probably licking his lips under his mask when he said, "I can tell this one's fear will be especially delicious."

A lady nodded. "I told you, a child's fear is more potent than an animal's. We should've been using kids in our recipe from the get-go."

Redhead disagreed. "The bugs, the rodents, and the birds were necessary test subjects. Without them, we wouldn't be where we are now."

Tall Man added, "Stay patient and vigilant, friends. Soon, the recipe will be just right, and our experiments will be over. We'll be making the big bucks before you know it. No more of this laughable cafeteria pay. Everyone will be lining up for a taste of our ice cream."

Steven couldn't believe he was getting all this on camera. Who should he show the footage to first? The principal? The police? His parents? His older brother?

The girl on the table grew weaker by the second. Soon enough, she was barely whimpering beneath the mask.

"There, there," a lady said to the girl. "Soon you'll hardly remember any of this, and you can rest at home for as long as you like."

This was why students were out of school "sick" for weeks! This was what had happened to Javy!

"She'll be resting all right," said Mr. Facial Hair. "That is, until we come for what's left of her."

The lunch staff laughed.

Steven wondered what that meant. "Until they come for what's left of her"?

They'd come for the girl at her home? Why? To keep her quiet, or . . . ?

A light bulb burst inside Steven's brain.

Javy had disappeared. His bedroom window had been left wide-open.

The cafeteria workers had come and taken Javy away! Kidnapped him!

But why? What was Javy's connection to this "ice cream recipe"?

What was going on?

"We all scream for ice cream," the lunch staff chanted together like a coven of witches. "We all scream for ice cream."

Steven's jaw dropped. He shook his head. No, they were saying, "We all scream for ice *scream*."

Behind Steven, something heavy and wet squelched against the floor.

He turned to find a giant pink blob heaving itself toward him, only a few feet away. The thing was taller than Steven and vaguely resembled a human being, with dripping arms and legs. Pieces of the monstrosity fell off in thick, gooey chunks, leaving a trail of viscous slime in its wake.

"*Stubbn...*" the thing moaned from a crooked hole in its sagging face. "*Stubbn... hupp muhhhh...*" A single human eye slowly slid down a mushy cheek.

As the thing reached for him, Steven yelped, fell back, and dropped his phone.

With both hands, Steven gripped the water pistol and fired hot sauce straight into the creature's malformed maw.

The thing sputtered as it said, "*Stubbn... isss muhhh... Hobbyyy... isss Hobbyyy...*"

"Hobbyyy"?

Javy!

That melting, pink horror show was... was... Javy?! Why did he look like that?!

Like... Like a giant mound of walking strawberry ice cream...

"Who left the freezer unlocked?"

"The new batch got loose!"

"There's some other kid over there!"

The lunch staff was suddenly around Steven and Javy-thing. Steven pawed the floor for his phone, found it, and sneaked the device into his rear pants pocket.

A lady pointed at the sentient pile of ice cream. "Get it back into the freezer before it completely melts and is ruined!"

With a couple of push brooms, Tall Man and Mr. Facial Hair moved Javy-thing further back into the kitchen. Javy-thing gurgled in protest, but away he went anyway, vanishing into the shadows.

Five women circled Steven. Each held a knife.

"Scream for us," one requested. "Let's see if you're worthy."

A different lady had a nastier idea. "If he doesn't squeal right, we should use him for mystery meat instead."

"No one wants to do mystery meat, Connie. Stop suggesting that."

Steven felt like screaming. For help. But he knew no one nearby would come to his aid. Nobody had saved the kids in the kitchen before him.

Steven felt like screaming. In terror. But he didn't want to give the lunch staff the satisfaction of breaking him down.

So he kicked out with both legs and connected with the nearest lunch lady's shins. The duct tape on his shoes did little to soften his blows.

The woman hunched over in pain, and Steven got her from point-blank range with hot sauce to the eyes. She howled and Steven shoved her into a pair of her evil sisters, knocking all three of them over like bowling pins.

Steven was on his feet now. Knives came his way from the fourth and fifth ladies, but blades were no matches for a water pistol wielded by an adrenaline-fueled marksman.

Soon, the final two women also cried hot sauce-laced tears.

Steven hurried off, following Javy-thing's trail of strawberry ice cream sludge, past the dazed girl strapped to the table. He found himself in a dark corner of the kitchen.

The only light came from a walk-in freezer with a wide-open door. Steven could hear the male cafeteria workers speaking inside to one another.

He could also hear Javy-thing pleading with them, "*Nuh-hh . . . nuhhh . . . dohnnn . . .*"

Steven stepped up to the freezer. He saw two other human-shaped mounds of ice cream in there, frozen solid. Tiny icicles hung from their bodies. They'd been there much longer than Javy-thing had. Large scoops of flesh were missing from their torsos.

The men with the push brooms had their backs to Steven as they struggled against their thawed-out prisoner. Javy-thing's drooping eye caught sight of his friend.

"Stubbn . . . Stubbn . . . hupp muhhh . . ."

"Help's coming, Javy!" Steven shouted.

The men turned to his voice, but Steven was already slamming the freezer door shut in their faces and tightly locking the outside latch. The lunch jerks weren't going anywhere.

From outside the freezer, Steven called 9-1-1. He wasn't dumb enough to think he could tackle this problem all on his own.

While on the phone with the emergency dispatcher, the lunch ladies found him, their knives out. But as soon as he said the police were on their way, the women scattered like frightened mice.

In the days and weeks that followed, various news reports focused on the cafeteria workers' nefarious deeds. Details about what they had been doing finally slithered out into the light.

For years, the cafeteria workers had grown resentful of lousy pay and ungrateful students, so they had worked together to create "ice scream," a delicious and addictive new dessert. Their hopes were that they could someday create a company and then sell their treat from inside their very own "ice scream shop".

The lunch staff had used a complex chemical mixture to manufacture a substance that, if inhaled, slowly altered the cells of affected organic matter. Basically, those unfortunate enough to come into contact with the "melting gas" would first show flu-like symptoms before eventually liquefying into one of three different ice scream flavors.

It was all very complicated scientific stuff that Steven didn't fully understand.

The lunch staff had first experimented on whatever vermin they could find running around the school. Over time, they had discovered that they could taste the "delicious fear" inside their victims, and that's when they began to focus on terrifying children.

The students with the most "impressive" screams were identified whenever they found disgusting surprises in their desserts during lunch. Those kids were then targeted and strapped to the cafeteria workers' "melting machine". Later, the children would be removed from their homes after their bodies began to break down and become dessert.

Quite a few students had to get counseling after learning they'd probably eaten some of their classmates for lunch.

Unfortunately, two of the lunch ladies were still at-large. But the rest of their colleagues had been captured and were in the process of being admitted to separate hospitals for the criminally insane.

After a series of surgeries and medications, Javy-thing's physical state had been mostly restored. So, now he was back to being just regular Javy. However, the poor guy never was quite the same again. He avoided sweets altogether, and his eyes and ears didn't quite line up like they used to.

A new lunch staff was eventually hired. Every day, baffled students were served heaps of vegetables and healthy vegan options.

Steven began to wonder if he had made a mistake getting rid of the old cafeteria workers. Especially when he began to notice his classmates' skin taking on a greenish hue.

And, was it just him, or was everybody's hair getting kind of leafy?

Wait. Did the brussel sprout on the end of his spork just blink at him?

Now that Steven inspected the other sprouts on his tray more closely, a couple of them did have brown, circular coloring in their centers. Almost as if they were dilated pupils . . .

Those steamed asparagus stalks were kind of strange, too.

Why did it look like they had fingernails curling at their ends?

BACKPACK ATTACK

THE BACKPACK WAS ALIVE.

Juan gulped as the pink bag shook in front of him. It hung by a single strap from Mallorie's chair, but it seemed ready to wriggle onto the floor.

Juan looked around. Did anyone else see this?

His sixth-grade English teacher, Mr. B, stood at the front of the classroom, jabbing a long finger at blood-red words on the whiteboard. The teacher said, "As you see, blah blah blah blah blah."

Juan's classmates focused on what Mr. B had written on the board and copied information into their notebooks. Juan glanced down at his own notebook. The only words he had written were his first and last names. Directly below those was a drawing of a medieval stick-figure army attacking a burning castle.

Juan's gaze centered on the backpack again. It wasn't moving. Had he imagined it?

At her seat in front of him, Mallorie hunched over, resting her blonde head on a fuzzy, purple sweater balled up like a small mountain on her desk. Juan couldn't see her face from where he sat, but he figured she was napping. That was good, because it meant the rest of the class would probably leave her alone.

Mallorie was different. Her clothes rarely matched, and her socks never did. Her shirt was usually stained by some snack, and her hair was always a tangled mess. She sang to herself, and kids did their best to avoid her, calling her "weirdo" or "freak". Rumors spread that she never showered, that she was covered in disease-carrying "cooties". It was easy to avoid Mallorie during class breaks and lunch, but during class, students had nowhere to hide. Juan's classmates refused to be near Mallorie, afraid that they would become "infected" with her cooties.

Mr. B had placed Mallorie on the far left of the classroom so that mean kids would be far enough away to leave her alone. But the distance didn't help much. Hurtful words sailed across the room just as easily as paper airplanes flew.

If Mallorie got out of her seat to sharpen a pencil, students cringed and shrieked in mock terror. If she raised a hand to answer a question, students would shout that her armpits stank.

Juan was one of the only kids who ignored Mallorie, and Mr. B knew that. That's why Juan sat behind her. Juan once tried to explain to his classmates that Mallorie didn't even smell very strange, but then gossip spread that he had kissed her behind the gym.

The backpack's front pocket bulged. Juan's eyes grew wide.

Scratch, scratch. A shapeless mass pressed against the zipper. *Scratch, scratch.*

The backpack wasn't alive. Something was trapped inside. And it wanted out.

Juan's palms were slick with sweat. What was in the bag? A rat? Hamster? Lizard?

Juan held his breath. Or could it be a snake?

"No, please, not that," Juan whispered.

Snakes had slithered and hissed through Juan's nightmares ever since his cousin David's birthday two years ago. That was when Randy the Reptile Wrangler came to entertain the guests. Randy brought with him geckos, amphibians like frogs and toads, and even a two-headed lizard, but his main attraction was a twelve-foot albino Burmese python named Diablo.

Juan was one of the first in line to handle the serpent. The snake was heavy on his shoulders, almost as heavy as his little sister when they played chicken-fights in the pool against their cousins. Mom took a photo, and then the snake wrapped its tail around Juan's throat. It squeezed. Constricted. Almost choked the life right out of him.

Juan never wanted to see another snake for as long as he lived.

Scratch, scratch. The backpack squirmed again. Perhaps Mallorie had smuggled Diablo's smaller brother into school. Juan rubbed his neck and shivered.

He raised his hand. Mr. B was writing something else on the board and had his back turned to most of the class. He missed Laura passing a note to Jessica three seats behind her.

"Hey, Mr. B!" said Juan, jumping out of his seat.

The teacher turned toward Juan. "Yes?" He looked at the boy from behind black, square-framed glasses. "Please, sit down."

But Juan didn't sit. He was too excited. "Mr. B," he said, "come here! Now!"

Juan had practically everyone's attention now. Mallorie still slept.

"What is it?" said the teacher. "And, please, sit down."

Juan shook his head. "No, you don't get it." He pointed. "Mallorie has something in her backpack."

"Cooties!" Gilbert cried.

Most of the class laughed. Mr. B crossed his arms and said, "Come on, people, let's be more mature than that."

"I think it's a snake!" said Juan.

A couple of the boys leapt from their seats, craning their necks to look across the room at the backpack. Some girls shifted uncomfortably behind their desks.

Mr. B sighed. "Calm down, calm down."

Luis said, "It's a cootie snake!"

A few people snickered, but Daisy said, "That's just dumb,

Luis."

Mr. B moved across the room, his bushy eyebrows raised. He stopped in front of Mallorie and said to Juan, "Now, what's going on?"

Juan looked to the backpack. It was silent and still. "There's an animal in there. Maybe it's not a snake, but something's moving around inside."

Mr. B said, "Mallorie told you this?"

"Yeah, did your girlfriend tell you?" shouted Kirk.

Mr. B gave Kirk a nasty look, and then locked his laser sights back on Juan. The teacher said, "You're not just making fun of Mallorie, are you? I thought you were better than that."

"No, I swear I saw something moving in there! I could hear it scratching, too!"

"Great." Mr. B rubbed his temples, and then he gently shook Mallorie's shoulder.

"Oh, no!" said Courtney. "Mr. B's infected!"

Mallorie suddenly shot up in her seat. Her blue eyes were bloodshot, and hair was glued to the right side of her face with drool. "What?" she muttered.

"Have a nice nap?" said Mr. B.

"Did you dream about being pretty?" said Kristina. "Because that'll never happen."

"Ooooooooooooooooooh!" most of the class said in unison.

Mallorie glared and screamed, "Shut up, jerks!"

"Hey, am I going to have to assign detention?" said Mr. B. "Kristina? Courtney? Kirk? Am I?"

The mean kids shook their heads. Kirk said, "Sorry, Mr. B."

Juan knew Kirk wasn't sorry in the least. None of his classmates were sorry. Most of them were jerks, just like Mallorie said.

Mallorie turned in her seat and saw Juan standing behind her. "What do you want?"

Mr. B said, "Juan thinks he saw an animal moving around in your backpack."

Mallorie burned Juan with her gaze. She bared her teeth like an angry mutt. "I don't have anything in my backpack, you idiot."

"Yes, you do!" said Juan. "It's trying to escape, but it's trapped!"

"What are you talking about?" said Mallorie.

"The freak's sister's in there!" yelled Luis.

"That doesn't make sense," said Tia.

"Her dog food lunch came to life!" Gilbert offered.

Students roared with laughter. Mr. B rubbed his temples again. "People, this isn't helping."

But the students kept laughing and shouting. Once sixth-graders go nuts, they stay nuts for a while.

Mallorie stood. "There's nothing in my backpack, Juan. Why would you say that, you jerk?"

Juan looked at Mr. B. "I ain't lying."

The teacher studied the boy's face. "You aren't lying."

"No, I ain't! Check that backpack, Mr. B. Please!"

Mr. B sighed and said to Mallorie, "Hand me the backpack, please."

"There's nothing in there," the girl protested.

"Please," said the teacher, holding out his hand. "Let me see."

"Why do you always let these jerks say mean stuff about me, Mr. B?"

"Just give me the backpack, Mallorie. Let's prove them wrong."

"Fine." Mallorie unhooked the backpack from her seat. Whatever was inside seemed to have fallen asleep or decided to play dead. There was no movement at all inside the bag as she handed it over to the teacher.

"Check the front pocket," said Juan.

Mallorie's eyes shot bullets at his face. She knew her smuggled secret was about to be revealed.

Most of the students now stood, craning their necks to get a closer look at the backpack. A couple of the less-courageous girls hid their faces in their hands.

"Oh, no, Mr. B!" Kirk said. "Now you've got Mallorie's

disease all over you, for sure! There's no cure!"

Half the class laughed, but Mallorie said, "Shut up, Kirk! Before I punch your ugly face!"

Mr. B shook his head. "There is no such thing as Mallorie's disease. No such thing as cooties. Don't let your imaginations get out of control. You guys are in the sixth grade. It's time you grew up a little here."

Between his thumb and index finger, the teacher gripped the backpack's front pocket zipper. Juan had a front row seat as the teacher slowly opened the bag. Others crowded around him.

"Be careful!" Daisy screamed. "Don't breathe in more of the disease!"

Mr. B said, "Enough, people, enough," but he was more focused on the backpack than the comments.

The pocket was now unzipped. The teacher began to pull it down a little to get a better look inside.

All Juan could see were shadows. The air seemed to grow thicker. It was as if Diablo constricted him again.

Then it attacked. Whatever it was.

It was a little larger than Mr. B's right hand. Juan knew this because the creature leapt out of the backpack and sat for a moment on the teacher's wrist. It looked like a furry, red lizard with a slender body and long tail. Except its face was like a monkey's. A monkey face with a pig snout nose and four bulging, cream-colored eyes.

The thing then sunk its jagged, needle-like teeth into the man's arm. And each of the creature's six legs had two sharp talons that dug deep into Mr. B's flesh.

The teacher dropped the backpack and screamed in pain. Girls screamed in terror. Boys screamed with glee.

Mr. B fell across Juan's desk, swinging his arm wildly, trying to free himself from the beast's bite. "Help!" he cried. "Get help!"

Maria went to the phone to call the main office, then hung up, saying the phone didn't work. It never worked.

Some students ran into the hall. Most stayed put, shrieking at the spectacle playing out at Juan's desk.

Mr. B grabbed the strange little animal with his left hand, trying to pry it from his arm. It only bit down harder. Blood began to squeeze between the creature's purple lips.

"Mallorie, what is that thing?" yelled Juan.

The girl was speechless. She just stared at the monster with hands over her mouth.

The beast squeaked and snarled as it settled jaws and claws deeper and deeper into the teacher's arm. Mr. B made no progress on tearing the monster away.

So Juan lifted his pencil from his desk and stabbed the creature in its leftmost eyeball.

The creature's lips released their hold on the teacher. The beast wailed and dropped onto Juan's desk. Three eyes stared up at the boy. Fangs opened, ready to strike.

Juan had the pencil ready to stab again. Why couldn't it have just been a snake?

"No," a voice commanded.

Juan thought he had said it at first, but he realized he had been too scared to speak. It wasn't Mr. B, either. The teacher bent over, clutching his bleeding arm, cursing, not even looking at the creature.

"No, cutie," said Mallorie. "Stop it."

The monster turned its head to look at the girl. It squeaked peacefully.

Mallorie now held the backpack in her hand. "Get back inside," she said, opening the front pocket as wide as she could.

The creature stared at her, eyes unblinking. It seemed to be confused.

"Now, cutie," said Mallorie. "Get back inside with the others."

"Others?" said Juan. "There are more?"

"Two more," she said.

"What the heck are they?" said Gilbert.

"My friends. My cuties."

"But what are they?" Courtney wondered. "Aliens?"

"No. I don't think so. They just showed up one day. They go everywhere I go. My cuties."

"I don't believe it . . ." Mr. B said. He stared at the monster. "It's true, Mallorie."

"What?" she said.

The teacher looked around the room at all his students. "Everyone said you had them . . . I didn't believe it."

"I don't get it," said Luis.

"What she calls 'cuties,' you call 'cooties.'" Mr. B looked back at the creature. "I don't know how it's possible. You said it enough—you all believed it enough—that it came true. Mallorie really has cooties."

Juan scratched his head. If he believed that Santa Claus was real, would the jolly fat man visit on Christmas?

The beast hissed at Mr. B. Mallorie took a step between creature and teacher. She said, "No, they're cuties. My friends. No one was supposed to know."

Mallorie brought the backpack closer to the animal. The bag wriggled in her grasp. "Come on, cutie," said the girl. "Your brother and sister are awake now, too. That isn't good."

"Don't open your backpack!" Juan pleaded. "Keep the other pockets closed!"

"We don't want to get eaten by your sisters, freak!" said Luis.

Kristina agreed. "They do look like her, don't they?"

"Shut up!" said Mallorie. "My cuties are already angry, jerks!'"

Mr. B said, "Who went for help?"

Kirk said, "Isaac and Lamont and Drake."

"Where'd they go?" the teacher said. "They could have just gone to Mr. Moore's! His room is across the hall!"

The creature shrieked once more, agitated by all of the raised voices. Its eyes focused on the teacher again. It leaned forward on two of its legs, talons spread out, ready for launch.

Mallorie picked it up by the base of its neck and placed it squirming back into her pink bag. She zipped up the front pocket. The backpack shook in her hands.

"Be quiet," she calmly said to the bag's lively contents.

"Give me that," said Mr. B, snatching the backpack away from Mallorie by one of the shoulder straps. "We can't have these things in here any longer."

"No!" cried Mallorie. "Mr. B!"

The teacher went for the door.

"Jump on the backpack!" said Courtney.

"Squash them!" yelled Gilbert.

"Burn them alive!" said Kristina.

Daisy nodded. "Good idea!"

"I have a lighter!" said Luis.

The classroom fell silent. The only sounds came from inside the backpack.

Luis's cheeks grew as red as tomatoes. "I mean, never mind. No, I don't."

Mr. B stopped at the doorway, blood dripping down his arm and plopping onto the tiled floor. He said, "People, please. I need you to stay calm and cooperate."

"Kill them!" screamed Kirk. "Kill those things!"

A few of the students began to chant, "Kill them! Kill them! Kill them!"

Juan's heart sank into his guts. Mr. B was hurt. Tears streamed down Mallorie's face. The class was rowdy. All of this was his fault.

Mallorie turned to her chanting classmates and pointed a trembling finger at them. "I hate you all!" she screamed. "HATE YOU! What did I ever do to you? HUH? Tell me what I did!"

"Mallorie . . ." Mr. B began. The creatures hissed inside the backpack.

"No," Mallorie sobbed. "They tell me, and they tell me NOW. Why do they think they can be like this? I've done nothing to them!"

Everyone in the room was quiet for a few seconds until Kristina said, "You're just . . . weird."

"Really weird," said Daisy.

"And ugly," said Kirk.

Juan knew he shouldn't have been so shocked by the laughter that followed Kirk's comment. His classmates never stopped.

"People, please!" said Mr. B.

Mallorie muttered something under her breath.

"What?" said Gilbert. "We can't hear you, freak."

Luis said, "You have something else to say?"

Mallorie said it again. This time it was loud enough for Juan to understand.

"Jerks."

She said it again, louder. "Jerks."

Again. Still louder. "Jerks!"

Again and again, each time louder than the time before it. "Jerks! Jerks!"

And then she screamed it one last time. "JERKS!"

Daisy screeched. She held her left arm out in front of her. It shook uncontrollably. Her right arm began to quake.

"Help me!" she said. "I can't stop!"

Then, she fell to the side, smacking her head on a desk on the way down. She hit the floor like a sack of flour. Her whole body shook while she whimpered next to Tia's feet.

"No!' shouted Mr. B. He raced for Daisy, dropping the backpack.

Gilbert and Luis began to shake and shriek at the same time. They fell.

Kristina and Kirk shuddered and tumbled.

The other students yelled. Juan let go of the bloody pencil and heard himself say, "What's happening?"

"I don't know!" Mr. B screamed beside Daisy. "Help! Get help!"

But as kids ran for the door, they froze in their tracks, quaking and falling, quaking and falling.

Juan watched Mallorie go toward the door, and he thought she might be going for help, but instead she stooped to pick up the backpack. A smile crept over her lips while she looked back at the class.

Had she somehow done this? She had, hadn't she? But how was that even poss—

Juan's body stiffened. His knees and elbows locked. His spine straightened, and his eyes popped open wide. He weakly moaned as his body took on a life of its own and violently shivered. His tongue quivered, a possessed worm inside his mouth.

"No," he said as some invisible force pulled him to the floor and caused his limbs to flail out of control. He stared at the ceiling and listened to his classmates cry, fall, and scream all around him.

His left hand smacked against the leg of a chair. His right foot kicked a desk over, sending textbooks and schoolwork to the floor.

Juan was a puppet. His mind worked just fine, but his body jolted back and forth, up and down, and he couldn't stop. He wanted to stop, but he couldn't.

Mallorie truly believed he was a "jerk". Now he had to suffer, jerk, and twist around just like everyone else.

The girl appeared above Juan. She looked down at him and grinned.

Scratch, scratch. The backpack squirmed and squealed in her hands. *Scratch, scratch.*

"M-Mallorie ... s-stop ..." Mr. B somehow forced out from his own spot on the floor a few feet away.

The girl knelt over Juan. She placed the backpack onto his heaving chest. "You wanted to see what was inside my backpack, right? Want a closer look?" Her eyes were those of a predator.

Juan could hear her slowly unzip the bag.

His brain tried to scream to her, "No, please, no!"

Mallorie giggled and said, "This is Juan, cuties. Chew his face off."

DEAD RIGHT

T'HE HISTORY TEST IN front of Vanessa asked a couple of questions about "feudalism," but the seventh-grader couldn't even define the word. Paying attention during class would have certainly paid off now, but passing notes to, and talking with other students was always easier and more fun. As for studying— that was something Vanessa never did. Reading a textbook and making flashcards? Yeah, right. Too boring and painful.

Now there were only forty-three minutes left in the period, and Vanessa had done little more than write her name at the top of the page and imagine rude answers to questions on the exam.

Question 2 said, "The 'Middle Ages' in Western Europe included the period when..." and Vanessa nearly wrote, "*Easy! That's when Mr. Huntley lost all of his hair. During his Middle Ages!*"

Question 9 read, "The epic poem, *Beowulf*, featured a monster named..." and Vanessa wanted to answer, "*The monster's name is Marysa. Scary, ugly, fat thing.*"

Vanessa smirked. Marysa Flores sat on the other side of the room, her two huge eyebrows looking like fighting caterpillars on her pimply, furrowed brow.

Question 17 asked something about "serfs," which Vanessa sort of remembered as being something like "slaves." She quickly imagined her classmates as her "serfs," doing everything she ordered of them. And then there would be Mr. Huntley, the lowliest serf of them all, scrubbing Vanessa's shoes and writing all her essays for her . . .

Unfortunately, Vanessa found that her fantasy didn't last very long. She trudged back to the real world.

If she failed the test, Mr. Huntley would definitely call home and speak with Aunt Rosie. That would result in Vanessa's phone being taken away and possibly sold to a used electronics store. Aunt Rosie didn't understand failure like Mom had.

Ugh! Why hadn't Vanessa studied? Even for fifteen minutes?

Because the phone had called out to her like it always did. At best, Aunt Rosie would make Vanessa delete the device's games and social media apps right in front of her. At worst, Aunt Rosie would take the phone away altogether, probably until high school.

Vanessa's chest tightened. Her breathing became more labored. Her palms sweated. She closed her eyes and shifted in her seat.

There was *no way* she was going to let her classmates see a panic attack. Panic attacks were her secret, locked inside her real tight.

"I have to go to the bathroom," Vanessa blurted.

Behind his podium, Mr. Huntley shook his head. "Not during a test, you don't. You know the rules."

"But it's an emergency!"

"Sorry, Vanessa."

She was desperate and said, "It's a *girl* emergency, you know?"

The teacher sighed. "You used that excuse to leave class last week."

Some students snickered. Vanessa told them to shut up or else.

Mr. Huntley walked over to her desk. Quietly, he said, "Come on, Vanessa. Focus. You're running out of time, and you haven't even started."

"But—"

"Vanessa. Stop it. You're going nowhere." He tapped her blank test with a finger. "Do your best."

The man walked away and Vanessa felt like screaming. She wanted to tear the pages to shreds and run out of the room. The walls were closing in, and there was no escape . . .

"Do not worry. I can help you."

The voice was soft, almost a whisper. Vanessa looked all around her, but nobody was there, which Vanessa already knew, since Mr. Huntley had made her sit in the back corner away from the rest of the class.

She couldn't believe it. She was literally driving herself crazy over a dumb test.

"You are not imagining things."

The voice returned, louder this time. It clearly belonged to a girl. But absolutely no one sat or stood near enough to be the source. Nobody was even looking Vanessa's way.

"I am here, right next to you. But you cannot see me because I am a ghost."

Vanessa leapt out of her seat. The chair scraped loudly against the floor.

Mr. Huntley was at Vanessa's side in seconds. "Sit down," he said between gritted teeth.

"I-I can't sit there."

"Why not?" asked the teacher.

"B-Because . . ." The eyes of each classmate were on her. They smothered her, refused to leave her alone. She couldn't say a ghost was talking to her. She'd be known as the pathetic "Ghost Girl" for years.

"Look," Vanessa said, "can I just sit someplace else? Please?"

"No."

"Just for today? That's all I want."

"Vanessa . . ." She could tell Mr. Huntley was near the end of his rope.

"I'll finish the test. Really."

The teacher rolled his eyes. "Okay, fine. But this is your last chance." He pointed. "Sit over there behind Zamary."

Vanessa took her things across the room and plopped down in her new seat, ignoring Zamary's complaints.

She looked around her. No ghosts. Just annoyed classmates.

It had to be her imagination playing tricks on her. Panic was making her loopy, that was all.

Suddenly, the voice said, "Do not run away, Vanessa. I am not here to hurt you."

Vanessa stiffened in her seat. She knew it wasn't Zamary practicing ventriloquism.

"I am a princess from long ago," said the voice. "I understand the subject matter of your exam. I can see you need my help, and I am here to offer it."

Vanessa shook her head in disbelief.

The ghost said, "I have been helping students at this school since the day it was built. I wander the halls trying to right the wrongs I made in my life. It is my blessing and my curse."

Vanessa hurriedly wrote on her page: "*I'm not stupid. No princess ever lived in this town.*"

The ghost chuckled. "History is not always what you expect it to be. It can still surprise you." There was a long pause. "However, if you do not believe me, I can help another struggling student . . ."

Vanessa shook her head again. She wrote and underlined: "*WAIT!!!*"

"Yes?" said the ghost. "Would you like my assistance?"

Vanessa nodded. What else was she going to do? Randomly write wrong answers and fail anyway? What could it hurt, to listen to this so-called "princess"?

"A wise decision," said the ghost. "Please listen carefully."

For the next half hour, Vanessa hurriedly scribbled answers. The ghost even helped her to double-check her work before the bell rang.

"*THANKS!!!*" Vanessa wrote to the ghost.

"It was my pleasure," said the ghost. "Have a nice day."

After Vanessa erased all the comments she had made to the phantom, she handed her test to Mr. Huntley, and she prayed that her phone and its contents would stay in her possession. Without the apps, would life even be worth living?

The next afternoon, Vanessa sat alone in the back corner of Mr. Huntley's room. If the ghost returned, she was going to ask for help with Pre-Algebra.

For nearly an entire class period, Vanessa heard nothing from the friendly specter. With six minutes left until the bell, the teacher announced, "I graded yesterday's tests."

The voice was in Vanessa's ear again: "I am excited. Are you?"

Vanessa nodded. Had the princess been standing there all along, watching, waiting? Gooseflesh raised on Vanessa's arms.

Mr. Huntley said, "Overall, you guys did pretty well. Some of you really impressed me. So, keep up the good work."

Vanessa smiled and nervously clapped her hands together. Would the "A" on her test make the teacher suspect her of cheating?

Probably. But Vanessa would think of how to explain her amazing success. It wasn't like she hadn't gotten away with cheating before.

Vanessa was the eleventh student to receive her graded exam. She had been holding her breath in anticipation and nearly passed out.

She finally let out a deep breath, looked at the test . . . and shrieked.

Her score was "16/100," and Mr. Huntley had angrily written in red ink at the top, "*Maybe one of these days you will actually study!*"

"No," Vanessa squeaked. "What happened?" Tears welled in her eyes. Her stomach churned.

"That's what you get," the phantom taunted. The ghost laughed and laughed. "Maybe next time you'll think twice before talking trash about the dead."

Vanessa drew "*???*" onto the test. And then scribbled: "*WHY'D YOU MAKE ME FAIL?*"

"I'm Princess Holmes. Not *a* princess. Idiot."

Vanessa sank. Princess had never been one of her favorites. They had even taken swings at each other once in elementary school. Vanessa had gotten in some good licks, even though the other girl had been a more experienced fighter.

When Princess died in a car crash a few months back, Vanessa had—perhaps distastefully—vocalized some joy over the incident.

"You think you've got a way with words? Well, guess what, Vanessa. My mouth's always been a weapon."

Vanessa wrote into the margins of her test: "*LEAVE ME ALONE!!!*"

"Shut up. I'm going to be in your ear every day. Making you miserable. You better believe it."

"*NO!!!*" wrote Vanessa. "*I WON'T LET YOU!!!*"

Princess cackled. "Wrong answer, Vanessa. That was the *wrong answer . . .*"

Words began to form on Vanessa's paper. The letters took shape from an unseen hand. They were wet, made of blood, and running down the page.

Vanessa shook her head in disbelief as Princess scrawled out her gory message: "*I'M GONNA RUIN UR LIFE!!!*"

The ghost then drew a sinister smiley-faced emoji.

She giggled into Vanessa's ear as she wrote another line: "*UR GONNA WISH U WERE DEAD 2!!!*"

THE BLOODY EYE

IN THE MIDDLE OF English class, Taylor was ready to slap Sasha Cooper across the face.

Sasha kept kicking the back of Taylor's seat, and Taylor was ready to turn around, rake her fingernails across Sasha's cheek, and tell the girl where she could shove her overgrown clown feet.

But the students were supposed to be working quietly on the semester's final exam, and Taylor didn't want to earn any of Miss Shoemaker's ire by causing a scene. The teacher seemed to like Taylor, and Taylor didn't want to ruin that by stooping to Sasha's level.

But Sasha would. Just. Not. Stop.

The two girls had never been friends. To be honest, Taylor hardly knew the girl at all, but for weeks now Sasha had treated Taylor like an enemy. This was all because Sasha's boyfriend, Cameron, had supposedly checked Taylor out in the cafeteria, and Taylor had supposedly smiled back at him.

However, no smile ever occurred.

Taylor barely knew Cameron, had never really spoken to Cameron, and not for a single moment of her life even thought Cameron was cute. He was too short, made fart noises during

Homeroom, and claimed to hate reading. Gross.

Kick. Kick. Kick.

Taylor couldn't focus on her work. So, she turned to Sasha and glared.

The other girl grinned at Taylor. "What're you looking at?" Sasha asked.

Taylor glared some more and then went back to her test.

That's when she felt a sudden, sharp stabbing sensation in her left eye. It was an excruciating pain, as if a hot syringe had been jammed into her skull with no warning whatsoever.

She grunted like a beast struck by a hunter's arrow. She dropped her pencil and raised her hand to her eye, fully expecting to find a knife or shard of glass protruding from her face.

Nothing was there.

Taylor pulled her hand away, discovered her fingertips were slick and red. Her left eye, a burning wildfire, was useless now. She closed it tightly, feeling blood pool beneath the lid and trickle in tiny, crimson rivulets between her lashes.

"Owwww," Taylor muttered, her lips quivering.

Sasha shushed. The nerve of that girl! All Sasha did was talk. If speaking non-stop were an occupation, Sasha could operate an entire chatterbox factory.

Because the students were taking their final, Sasha had for once decided to be focused and quiet. As if she had any chance of passing the class.

Taylor gripped the edge of her desk and forced herself to her feet. All she wanted to do was curl up into a pathetic, little ball and hide from the nightmarish pain.

Then, the horrible sting mercifully ripped away from her eye. There was a moment of relief for Taylor, a split second when she thought it was all over.

Until the pain came back twice as strong, now in her belly. Good thing Taylor had steadied herself against the desk, because without the support, she would have fallen over.

Had she been shot? Had an alien with a million teeth

burrowed into her stomach to chew on her guts?

With a shaky hand, Taylor pressed a palm against her abdomen. Again, she found no dagger, no stake, no spear, but her fingers were bloody. There was a hole in her shirt, a small but gory wound above her belly button.

Was she being attacked by a ghost with an invisible weapon? A silent insect with a mutant stinger?

"Sit down," ordered Sasha, as if she were some kind of angel who always stayed her in seat.

Taylor had the urge to throw up. Puke was coming fiery and fast, and she thought about turning to Sasha and spewing molten bile across the girl's loud and annoying face.

However, the vomitous feeling vanished in a flash. Taylor's stomach settled. She gulped in air like a dying fish, attempting to keep her rubbery legs tall and steady.

Explosive agony then tore through her lower back, near her spine. Taylor screamed, futilely reaching for a blade she knew would not be there.

Weak and weary, she fell to the ground, grisly tears staining her left cheek and the tiled floor a dark rose color. The poor girl shrieked like a slaughterhouse hog.

"Help me!" she pleaded again and again. "Please!"

Sasha watched Taylor writhe on the floor like unfinished roadkill. The motormouth didn't say a word, but she sure did snicker.

Penn and Danielle were the next two closest classmates to Taylor. They called out for Miss Shoemaker as others sprang from their seats for a closer look.

How could the teacher be so oblivious?

Behind her desk, Miss Shoemaker smiled, licked her lips. She didn't even cast a glance toward her students. Behind thick frames, the woman's eyes were downward, focused on something in her lap.

"Miss Shoemaker!" the kids cried. "Miss Shoemaker! Help her! Something's wrong with Taylor!"

Hearing the name of a star pupil snapped the educator to full attention. She removed herself from her comfortable chair and walked to the front of the room to get a clearer view of the chaos. The woman smiled no more. Concern lined her smooth face.

In her hand, the teacher held a doll, crudely constructed from string and straw. Also, something silver glinted beneath the classroom's glaring fluorescent lights.

"Taylor?" the teacher choked out. "Oh, no. No, no, no."

She looked at the strange object in her grasp. At its black button eyes. At a strand of brown hair duct-taped to its disproportionate head.

At the long, shiny needle shoved deep into the back of the handmade figure.

"I'm sorry," squeaked Miss Shoemaker. "I thought it was Sasha screaming. Not you, Taylor. I'm so, so sorry."

The woman removed the small spike from the doll. She went to the fallen girl, knelt down beside her. She directed Penn to go get the nurse.

Miss Shoemaker then ran her free hand through Taylor's long hair, examining it like an inept private detective who had forgotten her magnifying glass at home. The teacher shook her head as she compared the girl's mane to what was attached to the doll's noggin. The woman apologized again.

She glowered at Sasha. "I thought it was yours," said Miss Shoemaker. "Your hair I found on the floor."

"What?" Sasha was confused.

The educator rose to her feet, towering over the student, pointing a shaky finger at the dumbfounded girl. "It was supposed to be you! Not her! You!"

Miss Shoemaker cracked, giggled. Caught herself. Cracked again. Laughed louder.

"You, Sasha, you!" the woman exclaimed. "You did this! Do you see how you've pushed me? What you've *done*?"

Sasha was puzzled. She scratched her head, a sharp nail raking through her hair. She was actually speechless.

Taylor whimpered. Most of her pain was gone, but some still lingered like a shark circling a sinking ship.

She stared up at the teacher. Who was this person standing above her? This stranger she thought she knew? Someone good simply forced over a knife's edge? Or a secret psycho finally freed of her straitjacket?

Taylor's bloody eye would never see things the same way again.

THE EMACIATED MAN

DANIELLE COULDN'T BELIEVE SHE was actually doing it. She was ditching class for the first time.

As the girl walked through the darkness of the school's auditorium a few steps behind her friends, her heart did its best to beat a hole through her chest. The overanxious organ seemed to be telling her the same exact thing her brain was saying:

What in the world are you doing here, young lady?

If she, Melanie, and Beth were caught, it would definitely mean phone calls home. Absolutely detention. Possibly suspension. Maybe even black marks on their permanent records.

Melanie said, "Danielle, hurry up, you snail!"

Beth added, "What's done is done. Come on!"

Danielle couldn't really see her companions, but she could make out their cell phones (which they always had in-hand) floating like brightly lit specters in the gloom. They zoomed down the eerie center aisle of the cavernous room, toward the stage, away from the gleaming red exit sign.

For a moment, Danielle toyed with the idea of sprinting for the exit and racing to P.E. after all. She'd explain to Mr. Gomez why she was so late. Something about a lost notebook, perhaps.

Or an unscheduled trip to the nurse.

But how would she explain running away to Melanie and Beth? They'd never let her hear the end of it. She'd be a wimp, a baby, a disloyal *loser* forever.

For weeks, they'd been trying to convince her to skip class with them. It was an activity the pair had been taking part in more and more frequently. The duo didn't care if they were caught, if they disappointed their families any further. It wouldn't bother them in the least if they didn't culminate at year's end across the very stage they journeyed to that afternoon.

Danielle took another moment to think about why these girls were even her friends. Just because they'd all been "close" since third grade? Lately, they hadn't even really spent any quality time together outside of school.

Sure, Melanie and Beth slept over at each other's places still, but neither ever bothered to invite Danielle. Not that she was really into what they were likely doing, anyhow: drugs, alcohol, and endless hours of online foolishness.

Danielle halted in the middle of the auditorium. Would real friends pressure her to do something that made her feel so uncomfortable?

The realization was immediately accompanied by an overwhelming sense of fear. She had no other friends.

If Danielle didn't have these two, who did she have? Other "nerds" from her Honors classes? Yeah, they were nice kids for the most part, but she didn't want to give Melanie and Beth any more reason to mock her.

When it came down to it, Danielle wanted to hold on to what she had. Even if it was only a sliver of something special, a broken piece of the past that couldn't ever again be what it had once been.

"Move it, Danielle!"

"What's taking so long?"

Danielle snapped out of her funk. The other girls were already on the stage. Her eyes had now adjusted to the lack of light.

She could see them waving her over.

Melanie and Beth had both just had Drama with Ms. Young. They'd propped open one of the auditorium doors to allow them all easy access inside after the teacher went across campus to teach English.

Apparently, the girls had "something cool" to show Danielle. She figured it was a little drug stash. She didn't wish to partake, but if they wanted to, she wouldn't snitch.

Danielle forced herself toward her friends. They beckoned for her to join them, and then they disappeared between monstrous closed curtains.

"Hey!" she cried. "Wait!" She imagined all kinds of horrible creatures staring at her from the shadows.

She couldn't get to the others fast enough now. Danielle sprinted up the small staircase that wound up the side of the stage. She pushed through the curtains, choking on a cloud of dust.

Once through, she was blind again. Somehow, it was even darker back here.

A cell phone blinked to her right. "This way," said Melanie.

"You've got to see this," said Beth.

Danielle nodded, went to them. The girls crouched in a corner, behind a teetering stack of cardboard boxes. They illuminated the floor with their phone screens.

Large, choppy block letters were scratched—no, *carved*—into the wood.

"What's it say?" Danielle asked.

Melanie moved aside. "See for yourself."

Danielle crept forward. She squatted next to Beth, who held her cell above the words like a lantern.

A macabre message was scrawled into the stage: "R.I.P. DANIELLE DELGADO".

Danielle stood, shocked at the sight of her own name. "Who . . . Who did this?"

Beth brought her glowing phone up to Danielle's confused

face. "Look at her, Melanie. Priceless!"

Melanie smirked. "Yeah."

Beth pulled the phone away and said, "*We* did it, Danielle."

Melanie whispered directly into Danielle's ear. "I did the 'R.I.P.' Beth did your name."

Danielle's eyes once again adjusted to the darkness. "Why? This . . . This isn't funny, you guys."

Beth stood beside her, leaned in too close for comfort. "Well, it's funny to us. But we didn't really do it for your approval. We did it for *him*."

Danielle backed away from the girl's hot breath. "For who?"

Suddenly, Melanie was in her face, grinning like a serial killer. "We did it for The Emaciated Man."

Danielle raised an eyebrow. The Emaciated Man? Wasn't he a fictional character from the Internet? A tall, thin bogeyman who supposedly ate children? Someone's twisted creation whose image was photoshopped into pictures to give little kids nightmares?

Melanie turned to Beth and said, "She doesn't get it."

Beth laughed. "How could she? She's not special like us."

Melanie cackled. "True, true."

"What're you guys talking about?" asked Danielle.

"We're tired of this world," Beth explained. "We're going to be his servants and live with him in luxury."

"Servants of The Emaciated Man? But he's not real."

"Yes, he is!" Melanie screamed, and she shoved Danielle backward.

The girl fell into the leaning tower of boxes, plowing through them, spilling musty theater props into the shadows. Her head smacked against the hard stage. Small, shiny starbursts exploded before her eyes.

Dizzy, Danielle tried to stand, but Melanie kicked her in the ribs. Beth giggled like a hyena on helium when Danielle crumpled facedown against the floor.

Melanie said, "We asked around about him online. He found

us in a chatroom and has been talking to us for a while now."

"He's even Skyped with us a couple of times," said Beth.

Danielle couldn't believe it. They were out of their minds. Even if they did chat or Skype with someone, it was probably just a creep in a mask trying to lure stupid girls into some kind of sinister trap. These two had fallen for it.

Melanie said, "He needs a sacrifice."

"That's you," Beth said.

Melanie brandished a butcher's knife. Danielle cried out and began to crawl away.

She didn't get far. Melanie sat atop Danielle's back, pinning her to the stage. Danielle gasped for breath and struggled to break free, but Melanie refused to budge.

"Just do it already," said Beth.

"Okay, but stab her where?"

"No!" Danielle shouted. "Let me go!"

"In the back," Beth suggested. "Or through the heart."

"Why do I have to go first?" Melanie wondered. "You have a knife, too! *You* go first!"

Danielle lifted her head and pleaded, "Don't do this! Let me go! Please! I'm your friend!"

Beth stepped in front of her and sighed. "Oh, Danielle. We stopped caring about you a long time ago."

Danielle now saw a long blade in Beth's hand.

"Help!" Danielle shrieked. "Help! Someone, help me!"

Melanie smacked her head. "Shut up. We're alone. No one's going to hear you."

This only made Danielle scream louder. Then, sharp steel pressed against her throat, immediately putting her on mute.

Melanie yelled in her ear. "I said, 'Shut up'!"

Something warm and wet dripped onto one of Danielle's trembling hands. For a moment, she thought that Melanie had gone through with it, that she'd been stabbed. But Danielle felt no pain.

Melanie said, "Beth, my nose is bleeding. A lot."

Beth shrugged. "Well, did you let her hit you, or what?"

"No!" Melanie insisted.

Beth brought a hand up to her own face. "Oh." Rivers gushed from her nostrils, as well. "Oh, no."

Surging volts of electricity tore through Danielle's brain. She thought for sure that this time she'd finally been skewered. But, no, it was merely a mind-splitting headache. Her snout stung as it, too, hemorrhaged like an unruly faucet. Blood spewed onto the scarred floor.

"He must be here," said Beth. "We got bloody noses when he Skyped us, remember?"

Melanie replied, "Yeah. But we haven't even killed her yet. Why's he here already?"

The girls froze as heavy footsteps thundered on the other side of the curtains.

"**Greetings, my children,**" a voice hoarsely whispered. Danielle didn't hear it with her ears. Instead, it rattled deep inside her head. "**You have brought me into your darkness with you, just as we discussed.**"

Pale fingers resembling giant crab legs parted the curtains. An impossible figure in a sable suit stepped through.

The Emaciated Man. He *was* real.

He was completely bald with a blank ivory skull. No eyes, no nose, no ears, no mouth. Only smooth white space. He was freakishly thin, hence his name. And he was unnaturally tall, sure to dwarf any NBA player from past or present. At least ten feet from his crown down to his gigantic polished shoes.

Danielle shook her head in disbelief. She wanted to scream but could only muster a pathetic squeak.

The other girls didn't seem to notice. They stared up at the monster and beamed. Beth dropped to her knees and bowed to him.

"**Stand, my child,**" he said, and she did.

Then he was before them. The Emaciated Man cocked his head toward Beth, then toward Melanie, as if looking at them with invisible peepers.

"**All I needed to know,**" he said telepathically, "**was that you would go through with the deed.**" Each word made their noses bleed more. "**Be proud. You have proven yourselves to me.**"

"Thank you," said Melanie.

"What now, Master?" Beth pointed to Danielle. "What do we do with her?"

"**Do not fret, for today I am the one bringing the blood. Release the girl to me.**"

"No," Danielle squeaked. "No . . ."

Melanie's weight lifted off her. The knife's blade lifted, as well. Danielle had been hoping for a moment like this.

She pushed herself to her feet and ran like the wind.

But only for a few strides. The Emaciated Man's elongated legs soon took him around her. In no time, he had blocked her escape.

"**Now, now,**" he said. "**You really must stay.**"

He scooped up Danielle with one of his arms and pressed her close against himself. The creature smelled like charcoal burning under a hot grill.

Danielle attempted to break free of his hold, but he was much stronger than he looked. His slender arm looked as if it would break as easily as a twig, but it was an immovable vise.

The girl tried to shout for help again, demanded to be put down. The Emaciated Man only held her closer, muffling her voice to a helpless whisper.

"Master?" said Melanie. "Are we leaving now?"

"**Not until I feed. As you can imagine, I am only able to feast so often.**"

Danielle sobbed uncontrollably, not that anyone could hear her. She knew this was the end of her road. She'd never get to kiss a boy, go to college, become a lawyer . . .

"How do you eat?" Beth asked The Emaciated Man.

He said, "**Good question. I need a mouth, do I not?**" The beast held a skeletal hand out to Beth. "**Your knife, my child.**"

Beth stepped forward, giving him the weapon. He brought it to his face, seemingly inspecting it. Then, he pressed the knife's point against his milky bone.

"I must fashion a smile. I will shape my own, just as you would design a jack o'lantern's grin."

"Cool," commented Melanie.

"How many teeth should I have?"

"Countless," Beth offered. "Like on a chainsaw."

Melanie said, "And make them even sharper than a chainsaw's!"

"So it will be."

The Emaciated Man jammed the knife into his face, all the way to its hilt. Blood did not flow, because whatever the monster was, it did not bleed the way normal men and animals do. As he sliced his sinister smile, putrid, black sludge slowly oozed down the brute's chin, plopping onto Danielle's head, dripping into her eyes.

"This is so awesome," Melanie said as she raised her phone and took a quick snapshot of her "Master".

The phone's flash caught him off-guard. He pulled the knife away, turned to Melanie and snarled with his half-formed, jagged maw.

"NO!" he roared. His voice now came from the crooked hole in the middle of his face.

The Emaciated Man brought Beth's blade down like a lightning bolt. The weapon plunged through Melanie's left foot, pinning her to the stage. The stunned girl stared downward in silence for a second. She then dropped her phone and knife, finally letting loose shrieks of terror.

The monster snatched the phone from the floor and crushed it within his hand just as a toddler would a cookie.

He sprinkled the crumbs over Melanie. **"NO MORE!"** he bellowed.

"She's sorry," Beth said. "Right, Mel?"

The other girl was so focused on her pain that she could do

nothing but cry and scream. The Emaciated Man chuckled. "**I do not need her apology,**" he said, calm. "**Words are meaningless. I require action, child.**"

Beth nodded. "Okay, whatever you say."

"**Now, you, destroy *your* crutch,**" demanded the beast.

Beth looked at the phone in her own palm. She hesitated. Her hand trembled. "Do I have to?"

"**YES! DO IT NOW! Technology is useful to lure your witless kind but is a nuisance once I stand before you!**"

The girl gingerly placed the phone onto the stage. She closed her eyes, presumably holding back tears. Beth brought her boot down on the phone's screen again and again, shattering it. The device sparked as it lost its life.

The Emaciated Man smiled. "**Good. Obedient. Like a dog. Now, bring me her blade.**"

"What?" Beth's mouth dropped.

"**DO NOT QUESTION ME!**"

Danielle didn't blame Beth for her reluctance. There was no telling what the monster would do now. Surely, she regretted calling him here.

Beth's arm quivered as she brought the knife to The Emaciated Man. She walked by Melanie, who begged for assistance.

"**Thank you, dog.**" The creature took the knife in his hand. "**You are a true fool.**"

He smashed the knife through Beth's right foot, fixing her to the stage next to Melanie. Both girls howled in unison.

The Emaciated Man placed Danielle gently down onto her feet. "**I will not hurt you,**" he told her. "**Most do not find out until it is too late, but I feed only upon evil. It is where I get my strength. Goodness does not sit well in my stomach.**"

Danielle was in awe. The beast had spun a cunning web and drawn her "friends" into his trap. Melanie and Beth seemed less happy to learn this. They pleaded for their lives.

"**I am your fate,**" said the monster. "**This is the choice you made. I am the consequence of your ugliness.**"

He hooked his fingers into the corners of his mouth. He pulled back on his ragged lips, tearing the hole open even wider. To Melanie and Beth, he said, "**The better to bite you with.**" He ignored their screeching and spoke to Danielle. "**I am so very, very hungry. You do not want to see this mess.**"

He ushered her to the other side of the curtains, walked her to the steps at the edge of the stage. He placed a hand on her shoulder and delicately turned her to him.

"**You are my servant now,**" he said. "**I need you to find more tasty morsels. Will you lure them to me here in the dark?**"

Danielle thought about it for a moment. "No," she answered. "I won't fall for your trick like they did."

"**What do you mean?**"

"If I bring someone to you knowing that you'll kill them, I'm no better than Melanie or Beth. Then, you'll eat me, too. So, no, I won't be your servant."

The Emaciated Man smiled. "**Clever child. Intelligence gives me heartburn, anyway.**"

He released the girl. The monster disappeared back through the curtains to start his long-awaited meal.

As she raced toward the exit, Danielle held her hands over her ears. Melanie and Beth both cursed her name, but she never heard them.

She didn't hear their final wasted breaths, either, when they screamed for mercy as they were ripped to pieces by The Emaciated Man.

MIGHTIER THAN THE SWORD

FRUSTRATED, PENN THREW *The Collected Works of Edgar Allan Poe* across the room. The book opened and for a moment resembled a black bird in flight before crash landing onto the boy's bed, next to his pillow.

"Penn!" cried his little brother, Isaac, who had been standing in the doorway. "You can't treat it like that. Especially if it isn't yours."

The sixth-grader went to the bed and picked up the book, caressing it softly as if it were a wounded puppy. He inspected its yellowed pages, looking for any damage.

"I can't do this," Penn said, head slumped on his desk. "I'm not creative, and I don't even understand these stupid stories."

"You're lucky you didn't wreck this thing," said Isaac. "I would've had to pay a huge fine!" He paused. "Or given away my soul or something."

Penn rolled his eyes. "Come on. It's just a book."

Isaac shook his head. "This is the librarian's special copy. She keeps it locked in a safe under the checkout counter. She only let me borrow it for you because she trusts me, Penn."

Isaac was a bookworm who spent practically every free

moment at school in the library. He was a good kid, a great student, and an avid reader. Their parents said they were proud of both their sons, but Penn knew he was the one living in his brother's shadow.

"I think I'm allergic to reading," said the eighth-grader, wiping his nose with a sleeve.

"Yeah, right."

"Well, that dumb book is too dusty for me to read it, okay?"

Isaac sat on the edge of the bed. "Why do you always make so many excuses? All you have to do is try."

"I did try! I tried to read a couple of the stories in there, but it's all written in cursive."

"This is Edgar Allan Poe's personal copy! He wrote everything in here with his own hand!"

"It was giving me a headache."

"That's an excuse."

"What do you want me to say, Isaac? That I'm not as good at sounding out words as you? That I read those stories but can't remember any of them? I mean, let's be real. I'm just going to have to give up."

Isaac flipped through the book. "I really thought you'd give this a shot. You like horror, and Edgar Allan Poe wrote some pretty demented stuff."

"I like *watching* horror. Movies. Reading's not my thing."

Isaac shrugged. "I could help you if you let me."

Penn sat up straight. "Help me how?"

Isaac gestured to the film posters tacked to the walls. Penn's bedroom was plastered with monstrous imagery. Masked killers. Red-eyed creatures. Fanged terrors.

"Which ones do you like the most?" Isaac asked. "We can brainstorm what makes them so cool, and maybe then you'll get some ideas for your own scary story."

Penn sighed. He already felt like a loser for initially asking his little brother for help. Now Isaac was going to practically hold his hand through the entire assignment. Then again, Penn didn't exactly want to fail his Creative Writing class.

"All right," said Penn. "Help me out some more."

"Awesome!" Isaac was perhaps too excited, but it wasn't often that his brother asked to hang out.

Penn balled up his fists playfully. "I better get at least a 'B' on this story, or you're going to pay."

"Oh. Okay." Isaac gulped.

"I'm just messing with you, man."

Isaac grinned. "Well, yeah, sure. I knew that."

"So, my favorites, huh?"

Isaac nodded. "The ones you think about the most."

Penn crossed his arms, pondering how he'd answer. His eyes locked onto the poster for *Eden's Plot*. A bald vampire with pale blue skin reached for the viewer. The beast's long claws sprang forth from the shadows of a dark, billowing cloak.

Penn said, "The movies I watched with Grandpa, then. You know, before he died."

"Right."

"He always said ... that when I turned ten ... he'd share them with me. 'His films,' he called them. And so he did. On my tenth birthday, we watched *Hugo* for the first time."

Both boys looked to the *Hugo* film poster. The titular Rottweiler stood on the hood of a car, thick foam dripping from his snarling jaws.

Penn continued, "We watched a few more movies after that. But then ... Grandpa got sick."

"*Hugo ... Eden's Plot ... Justine ... Agony ...*" Isaac pointed to posters. "Those are all based off Stewart Kang novels."

"Yeah."

"And that one: *Headless Horseman's Hollow*. That's based off an old story that's like two hundred years old."

"I know."

"You really never read any of those stories?"

"No. I don't like to read, Isaac!"

"Okay, okay. Sheesh. Relax." Isaac put a hand on his chin,

studying the vampire of *Eden's Plot*. "You like the antagonists, don't you?"

"The *antago-whats*?"

"The antago*nists*. The villains in these movies. The bad guys. The monsters."

Penn said, "Sure. Good horror movies have good villains."

"What else do you like about the movies?"

"They're bloody. Gory."

"Okay, you like the violence. Anything else?"

"That ... That *feeling* you get, you know? In your stomach? When you know something bad is about to happen to the good guy. That the antago ... the antago ..."

"Antagonist."

"That feeling that the antagonist might be hiding around the corner, ready to jump out and attack the good guy. I like that feeling."

"The feeling of suspense."

"Yeah, that's it." Penn grinned. "Suspense!"

"And good guys are called 'protagonists.'"

"Yeah, I think I remember Mr. Fairchild going over that in class."

Isaac said, "Well, when you write your story, include those things you like: a scary antagonist, some violence, suspense ... If you write what you like, it'll be easier. More fun."

"You're right. Yeah. Thanks." Penn struggled to get that last word out of his mouth.

"No problem," said Isaac. "Just help me get past the final mission in *Common Warzone 4*."

Penn laughed. At least he'd always be superior when it came to video games and sports.

His eye caught something sticking out of the book in Isaac's hands. He stood and walked over to the bed.

"Is that a bookmark?" said Penn.

"Bookmark?" Isaac didn't see it.

No, it wasn't a bookmark. Or was it? Whatever it was, it was dark, slender, and peeked out from the weathered spine of *The Collected Works of Edgar Allan Poe.*

Penn pulled the mysterious object free.

"A feather?" he said, confused, turning it over in his hands. "What kind of bird does this belong to? A crow?"

"Wow!" said Isaac. "Be careful with that. Who knows how long it's been hidden inside there!"

Penn scratched his head. "Why would a feather be here?"

"Are you serious? It's a raven's feather, Penn!"

"Okay, so what? That's the same as a crow, right?"

"No, it isn't," said Isaac. "But the significance of a raven to Edgar Allan Poe is that Poe wrote a very famous spooky poem called 'The Raven.'"

Penn slowly nodded. "Okay, I get it. Kind of."

Isaac carefully took the feather from his brother. "And it's not a feather, Penn. Well, it's not *just* a feather."

"Oh, yeah? What is it, then?"

"It's a quill. You see how it's pointed at the end? How it's sharp and darkened at its tip?"

"You're saying someone used to write with this thing?"

"Yep." Isaac beamed. "Man, this is so cool. This is probably Edgar Allan Poe's very own quill!"

An idea flashed inside Penn's head. "What if . . . ?"

"What if *what?*"

Penn rushed back over to his desk. He hurriedly pushed aside empty food wrappers and crumpled paper balls. Within a minute, he had retrieved six black ballpoint ink pens from the mess.

He unscrewed the bottom of each pen and pulled closer a small plate stained with ketchup and bits of cold hot dog. Penn emptied the ink from all of the writing instruments onto the dish.

"What're you—?" Isaac said before Penn snatched the quill from his grasp. "Hey!"

"Calm down, will you?" Penn dipped the pointy end of the quill into the dark, inky pool on the dish. "See? I'm going to use this to write my story. Cool, huh?"

"Yeah!" Isaac's eyes lit up. "Good idea! Just like Poe!"

With the quill in his hand, Penn almost felt like a writer. Like he could actually do the assignment.

He sat back in his chair. "All right, dork," he said to his brother. "Where do you think I should begin?"

The boys sat in silence for a while. Penn felt the frustration and doubt begin to creep back into his brain.

Then, Isaac said, "What if you borrowed some ideas from Stewart Kang?"

Penn's ears perked. "What do you mean?"

"Use characters and parts of the plot from Kang's work, but change them enough so that your story still seems original."

"I don't get it."

"You think that vampire from *Eden's Plot* is a good antagonist, right?"

"Correct..."

"Put a vampire like that one in your story, then."

"There are lots of vampires in *Eden's Plot*."

"Fine. Put *lots* of vampires into your story, if you want to. And also put other characters or things that Kang's used in there. You don't have to start from scratch. Borrow Kang's ideas. The ones that you already admire."

Penn waved his hand. "Naw, that's *plager . . . plager . . .* !"

"Plagiarism? Not if you change most of the characters somehow and maybe set the story in present day."

The rusty wheels inside Penn's brain spun with new life. His brother was on to something.

Within moments, the quill touched paper, and a tale began to take shape.

Penn opened his eyes to find his head on his desk. Drool had partially glued notebook paper to his cheek.

He bolted upright in his seat, glanced at the alarm clock, and scanned the room. He was alone. Isaac had left hours ago.

Penn's eyes had grown heavy around ten-thirty. He had

pushed through the sleepiness to finish his story. Or at least he had tried to . . .

It was now a little past midnight. The room was dark except for pale lamplight from his desk. The air was frigid. The window was wide open. Who had opened it? Isaac? But why? Neither of the boys liked the winter chill.

Penn shivered on his way over to the window. He reached up to the pane, and a screeching missile zoomed into the room.

No, not a missile. A huge, black bat, darker than night.

The creature hovered in front of Penn, leathery wings slapping at his face.

Penn didn't think bats got so big. The creature's body was over a foot long. Its wingspan was at least four times that size. Its ears looked too large for its head, like they were more suited to a fox's skull.

The bat shrieked, and Penn saw a pair of rattlesnake fangs in the animal's mouth. Saw venomous beads ballooning on the teeth's barbed tips.

Bats definitely did not have chompers like that.

Penn jumped back, putting some distance between him and the impossible animal.

The bat flapped over to Penn's desk and, with its clawed feet, snatched his scary story from the table.

"Hey!" shouted Penn.

He reached into his clothes hamper, removed a dirty sweatshirt, and stepped towards his desk. He swatted the bat with the sweatshirt as if the monster were a giant bug.

Penn reached for the story in the bat's clutches. The animal screamed at him angrily. They were now in a tug-of-war over the manuscript.

Penn swung the sweatshirt again and again. "Let go!"

The bat snapped its jaws at Penn, missing his left wrist by inches. Penn cried out and released the piece of paper. The bat began laughing at the boy.

The bedroom door opened. There stood Isaac rubbing sleep

from his eyes. "What's going on? You woke me up."

Isaac clutched the old Poe book close to his chest. Apparently, he had been holding it even while he slept.

His eyes went wide at the sight of the attacking bat. "Whoa! What's that?!"

The bat looked Isaac's way, and Penn grabbed the paper again.

"Help me!" yelled Penn. "Throw the book at it!"

Isaac hesitated. There was no way he was going to risk damaging the book. Instead, he yanked a pillow from the bed.

"Do something!" Penn pleaded. "But don't get too close! It's venomous!"

"'Venomous'? Bats aren't venomous!"

Isaac took a swing with the pillow. The bat grabbed a corner in its jaws and tore a hole through the thin fabric. Cotton stuffing pumped out.

Penn also saw bat-fang venom pump *into* the pillow.

Isaac let go on his end. The bat released the pillow, too.

The bat then yanked back on the paper, ripping it free of Penn. The animal turned to the window, screeched in victory, and swooped outside.

"No!" cried Penn. "I need to finish that!"

He and Isaac both ran to the window. But the bat was already flying through the moonlit sky.

They watched it land across the street and hang upside down on the rickety chain link fence that bordered the middle school.

In the bat's grasp, Penn's story fluttered in an icy breeze. The bat looked up at the boys in the window, taunting them with glowing, red eyes.

"I have to get that story back," Penn seethed. "I'm not about to start over!"

"It's past midnight," said Isaac. "You can't go outside. Mom and Dad'll kill you!"

Penn shrugged on the dirty sweatshirt he had used as a weapon and said, "If I fail Creative Writing, I'm dead anyway." He slipped his feet into weathered tennis shoes. "Don't snitch on me, Isaac. Please. I'll be right back. Real quick. I promise."

"No," said his brother. "I'm going with you."

"You are?"

Isaac nodded. "Let me go put on a jacket and my shoes." The sixth-grader disappeared into his bedroom next door.

Penn stood at the window, locked in a staring contest with the bat across the street.

How on Earth could that thing possibly be real?

He silently begged the beast to stay put.

Half a minute later, Isaac was back without the book. "Come on!" said the younger boy. "We probably don't have much time!"

The brothers crept past their parents' room. The door was tightly shut. Dad's bear-like snores had probably drowned out the ruckus in Penn's room.

Penn's hands sweated inside a pair of gloves. His heart pulsed more quickly than a hummingbird's heartbeat. If their parents caught them outside the house, who knew what the consequences would be?

"Shut up!" Penn scolded his brother, even though Isaac was completely silent.

Once past their parents' bedroom, the boys bolted for the front door. Penn unlocked it quickly. The brothers rushed into the cold night.

As they approached it, the bat cackled. Penn balled his hands into fists. They were a hundred feet away from the creature.

"That thing's huge," said Isaac. "And its teeth! I saw the venom, like you said! What kind of bat *is* that?" Isaac's bravery seemed to be waning by the second. "Shouldn't we call Animal Control?"

"This late at night? Plus, Animal Control doesn't deal with vampires, Isaac."

"V-Vampire?"

"Yeah. Like the one from my story."

"What're you talking about?"

"My story, it's about two brothers, late at night, running away from monsters."

"Okay..."

"I did what you told me. Used ideas from Stewart Kang's stories. But changed the details to make them more my own."

"What're you saying?"

"In my story, I wrote a vampire. Like the one from *Eden's Plot*. But my vampire turns into a giant bat. And it has venom, too. I wanted to make it really twisted. Really scary."

Isaac pointed. "You think that... that thing is from your story?"

"Sounds crazy, but yes!"

"How, though? How would it come true? How is it here?"

"I don't know!"

"And, if it's a vampire, how'd it get into your room? Vampires need an invitation, don't they? Isn't that how they work?"

No headlights approached, so Penn stepped into the street. Isaac was a couple of steps behind.

They were only fifty feet away from the bat now. Forty-five. Thirty-five. Thirty...

"Penn, did you invite that thing into your room?"

When they were twenty feet away, the bat somersaulted away from the fence, and, in mid-air, transformed into a full-grown man. He landed in a crouch on the sidewalk before the boys.

Isaac's eyes went wide. "Whoa!"

The vampire rose to a full six feet, wearing a sable suit, as well as a red cape with a raised collar. He had a pale, bald head and a goatee with stark white hair. He held Penn's story in a hand with yellow, dagger-like fingernails.

The vampire gazed down at the brothers, showing off a venomous smile.

"Hello, Penn. Hello, Isaac."

"G-Grandpa?" Isaac choked out.

"That's how he got into our house," Penn explained. "Because Grandpa's been there before."

"Maybe I should go back inside," said Grampire, "and visit

your parents."

Isaac clutched his brother's arm, pulling him back. "Penn?!"

"I . . . I made my vampire an old guy," said Penn. "Like the one from *Eden's Plot*. When I described him, I may have mentioned he looked just like . . . like that. Like Grandpa."

Grampire hissed at the boys.

Isaac tried moving them away from the thing with their grandfather's face. "Th-That's not Grandpa!" he declared. He made the sign of the cross with his index fingers.

"Are you serious?" asked the vampire. "That doesn't work."

Penn stood his ground. "Give me back my story!"

The monster chuckled. "I don't think so."

"Why do you want it anyway?" Isaac asked.

The monster did not reply.

"If he's even a little bit like Grandpa really was," Penn whispered to his brother, "maybe I can convince him to hand it over?"

Isaac shook his head. "Good luck with that."

Penn looked the vampire right in his red eyes. "You don't want this. For me to fail. Grandpa . . . you always told me school is important. That . . . That you wished you'd taken it more seriously when you were a kid."

Grampire looked to his left, past the fence, to Poe Middle. "School," he said, "is merely a horror movie from which you'll never escape."

"Told you," said Isaac. "Definitely not Grandpa."

"The story. I need it." Penn held out a hand. "Now."

"Perhaps." Grampire shrugged. "Since taking it has already served its purpose."

"What does that even mean?" Penn was getting angry. "What purpose? Just give it already!"

"This is the bait." Grampire turned the paper over in his hands, studying it. "You have come for the bait, which makes you the prey." He pointed behind the boys. "And they . . . they have come for the prey."

Penn and Isaac turned. Seven houses down, a trio of predators advanced beneath the streetlights.

On the sidewalk was a growling Rottweiler, his muzzle foamy and dripping.

Holding the dog's leash was a woman their mother's age. She wore a tattered dress under a flannel jacket. With her other hand, the woman gripped a claw hammer.

Rolling beside them in the street was a ghostly silent, black 1969 Ford Mustang. No driver was behind the wheel.

"Let me guess," Isaac said. "More antagonists you borrowed from Stewart Kang stories?"

Penn nodded.

"Great. Just great!"

There was Hugo, a rabid dog from the 1983 film of the same name.

Emmy Milk, an obsessive madwoman from 1990's *Agony*.

The Mustang, a bloodthirsty vehicle from 1983's other Kang adaptation, *Justine*.

Penn gulped. "I think it was all a trap to get us outside with them."

Isaac turned back to Grampire. "Well, that wasn't nice!"

The bloodsucker pointed to Penn. "Blame him. He wrote me this way."

"Thanks, Penn!" Isaac pointed back at Grampire. "I'm going to scream, and when I do, our dad's going to come right out here and kick your—"

Grampire lunged for Isaac, grabbing him by the arm. Isaac and Penn both screamed in protest as the monster pulled the smaller boy in for an unwanted embrace.

Grampire wrapped Isaac up inside his cape and then sank his fangs into the boy's neck.

"Isaac! No!" Penn watched his brother fall limp under the vampire's bite.

He then glanced back at the other three antagonists. The dog, crazy lady, and car didn't appear to be in any particular hurry to attack. They approached calmly, assuredly, and were only four houses away from Penn now.

The Rottweiler barked, spittle flinging through the air.

The Mustang revved its engine.

"We want an autograph, Penn!" Emmy Milk shouted. "We're your number-one fans!"

Grampire detached himself from Isaac and dropped the boy to the ground. The monster wiped his mouth dry, using the edge of his cape like a cloth napkin.

"A delicious snack," he said to Penn. "A little energy boost for me. A huge complication for you."

Grampire then leapt into the air, became the bat, and flew over the fence into Poe Middle School, the scary story still in his possession.

Penn slapped the fence in frustration. "WAIT! COME BACK!"

He raced over to Isaac, who lied in a patch of grass. Isaac's neck displayed a pair of puncture wounds. The holes didn't bleed, but bruising had begun to form around them.

Whether it got him grounded or not, Penn needed his parents' assistance.

"HELP!" Penn yelled. "DAD! MOM! HELP US! HELP!"

But the windows in their parents' bedroom remained dark.

"Doesn't hurt that much," Isaac said in a voice barely above a whisper. "Can't move, though. Everything's . . . numb."

The rattlesnake venom was taking hold of Isaac's body.

"I'm getting you out of here, okay?" Penn said. He yelled again, "HELP! SOMEBODY, HELP US! PLEASE!"

A Chihuahua yapped inside the house next door to theirs. It was Mr. Saint's dog, Pumpkin.

Hugo the Rottweiler barked back at Mr. Saint's front door. The trifecta of terror was nearly within striking distance of the boys.

"Got anything to write with, Penn?" Emmy asked. "If not, we'll take a signature . . . in blood!"

Penn wrestled one of Isaac's arms around his shoulders and

pulled the smaller boy to his feet. "Come on!"

Unfortunately, Isaac's legs buckled, causing both brothers to fall on their faces.

"No, no, no, NO!" Penn screamed. "HELP! THEY'RE GOING TO KILL US! HELP!"

That's when Mr. Saint stepped onto his porch. He wore a bathrobe and slippers. "What's going on out here?" Pumpkin stood at his feet, snarling at the scene.

"You were about to miss all the fun," Emmy replied from her spot across the street. "But now you can join in."

"Get away from those boys!" Mr. Saint took a couple of steps toward the woman. Pumpkin matched his stride.

Mr. Saint was also a horror film enthusiast. He always invited the neighborhood kids to help him decorate his front yard for Halloween. In other words, Mr. Saint had been nothing but kind to Penn and Isaac.

He certainly didn't deserve what happened to him next.

"Boys!" Mr. Saint walked across his yard. "Get over here, right now!" His Chihuahua seemed to call the brothers over, as well.

The villains turned in unison, their focus now on the neighbor and his dog.

A growl like rolling thunder rumbled inside Hugo's throat.

"RUN, MR. SAINT! RUN!"

Penn would have to handle the monsters on his own, after all. He didn't need to see the nice man hurt. Or worse.

"It's okay, Penn," said Mr. Saint. "It's okay."

Emmy snickered. "No, it's not." She unhooked Hugo from his leash and the enormous animal ran for Mr. Saint's lawn.

Brave, stupid, little Pumpkin met the Rottweiler halfway across the grass. The Chihuahua never stood a chance.

Hugo snatched Pumpkin up into his jaws and crushed the little yapper between his teeth. The Chihuahua yelped as he fell apart in ragged pieces.

Mr. Saint was practically on top of the Rottweiler now,

smacking the beast across the skull with his slippers. Hugo tossed Pumpkin aside, leaving what was left of the small dog to spurt next to a couple of lawn gnomes.

Hugo then spat a frothy stream of acid into Mr. Saint's eyes. Yes, in his story, Penn had given the killer Rottweiler the ability to wage chemical warfare.

Mr. Saint shrieked. Clawed at his face. He stumbled blindly, unaware that he was headed straight for Pumpkin's corpse.

"Oh!" was all he said when he stepped inside what was left of his dog. He slipped on exposed guts and pitched forward, right into Emmy Milk's swinging hammer.

The metal tool whacked Mr. Saint above his left ear, cracking against the man's head and sending him, dizzy, into the street.

That's where Justine, the pristine, possessed Mustang waited with her wipe-open hood. She drove into Mr. Saint with her front bumper, spilling him over her exposed engine.

Justine's hood then slammed shut, open, shut, open, shut, open, crushing Mr. Saint with a series of devastating "bites" as she "chewed" him alive. The hood eventually clamped down over the broken man with some finality, locking him inside the car.

Justine's engine revved, drowning out the man's screams. Mr. Saint's blood sprayed out of the Mustang's muffler, splattering the asphalt road with a grisly paintjob.

Penn instantly regretted giving the car a taste for human flesh.

He dragged Isaac along the sidewalk, away from the horrifying mess.

This was all Penn's fault.

Isaac's current condition. Mr. Saint's death. Pumpkin's demise.

If he hadn't written that story and brought these villains to life, everyone would still be okay. As much as he wanted to, Penn couldn't call out for any more help. He wouldn't put anyone else in harm's way. Especially his parents.

So, what could he do, then?

Isaac mumbled, "I don't feel good." He sweated profusely now. "Put me down. Please."

Penn propped his brother against the middle school fence. Isaac threw up all over himself.

In the distance, the vampire bat circled the middle school P.E. field. Still in the bat's grasp, Penn's story flapped in the wind. Penn suddenly knew what he had to do.

Destroy it.

Destroy the story.

Tear it to shreds.

If it no longer existed, neither would its characters. The villains would be destroyed, too.

Hopefully.

And if the antagonists were gone, no one would be able to stop Penn from getting help for his brother.

"Isaac," said the older boy, "I'll be right back." Penn wasn't sure if he was lying to the kid or not.

Penn moved closer to where the villains congregated, still in front of Mr. Saint's house. He had to lure the monsters away from Isaac and his vulnerable state.

Penn shouted, "Hey, over here!" He waved his arms above his head and then began to climb the middle school fence.

Hugo sprinted for Penn, jumping to tear a chunk out of his right leg. But Penn pulled himself away just in time. The dog's corrosive drool hit a couple of metal chain links, dissolving them apart, as if they'd been struck with lava.

Safely on Poe Middle School property now, Penn was off, running under the moonlight, headed for the vampire thief in the sky.

He looked back to see Hugo spit at the fence, melting a larger hole in its side. Soon enough, the Rottweiler would be right on Penn's heels.

Penn also saw Emmy Milk sitting in Justine's driver's seat. The Mustang lifted from the ground as a quartet of oversized horse's legs grew from where her tires once stood.

The legs were another addition from Penn's imagination. Something he'd hoped to never see come true.

No such luck. Penn cursed as Justine's literal horsepower propelled herself and her passenger over the fence in a single impressive bound.

"OhGodOhGodOhGod!"

Penn ran as fast as he could, but horse hooves thundered behind him, getting closer by the second. In moments, he'd be trampled flat.

He fell to his knees and curled into a ball as Justine galloped right over him. She turned around, engine growling and headlights illuminating Penn's trembling body.

She could've easily stepped on him. Simply squashed him like roadkill.

Why hadn't she?

"What?!" Penn shouted. "What do you want?!"

Emmy leaned out of Justine's driver's side window. "You've got a good head on your shoulders! You figure it out!"

Something orange glowed in Emmy's lap. Through the windshield, Penn saw her lift a fireball into her hands.

No. Not a fireball.

A *head*, on fire.

Mr. Saint's severed skull.

Emmy laughed maniacally and said, "Run, boy! Run!"

So he did. Just like that, the chase was on again, Emmy a twisted version of the Headless Horseman and Justine her nightmarish steed.

Penn ran, and the Mustang trotted after, deliberately staying on pace with him. Emmy giggled. They could've overtaken Penn in a second, but they were toying with him! Messing with Penn! They had to be!

Above, the vampire bat cackled, too. It could have easily disappeared over any number of rooftops, but the creature got some kind of twisted joy from leading Penn in circles around the field.

Penn raised a fist to the sky. "The story! I want it!"

The flaming head whizzed by his face, singeing his left earlobe. It rolled harmlessly across the grass like an errant soccer ball.

Only, this "ball" featured Mr. Saint's face forever frozen in terror.

Penn looked behind him, ready to tell Emmy that she needed to work on her aim, but she and the Mustang weren't there.

Instead, they had pulled up beside Penn, on his right!

Emmy leaned out Justine's window, swinging the claw end of her hammer down at the boy. Penn managed to dodge most of the blow, but the claw did catch his sweatshirt, ripping some of the fabric free.

"If you won't give me an autograph," Emmy said, "I'll give you mine!"

She swung the hammer again and again. Penn managed to duck each attack.

He put up his hands to shield his face, and on the fourth swing of the hammer, Emmy tore a jagged scrape along his right forearm.

Penn shrieked in pain. He fell to the ground again, this time cradling a wound.

The Mustang stood over Penn, ready to crush him with her front hooves. The car's engine roared.

"Do it," Emmy said, climbing back into the car's cab. "Put him out of his misery."

Justine reared back on her hind legs, about to smash Penn, when the vampire bat swooped in from nowhere and clasped onto one of the limbs, biting into horseflesh.

The car released a grating, metallic screech. Freaking out and in pain, she fell backward onto her trunk and then flipped onto her roof, caving in on top of Emmy.

Steel crunched. Glass sprayed.

What the . . . ?! Why'd the vampire have such a sudden change of heart?!

Because it wasn't the vampire. At least, not the big one still flying around in the sky.

This was a smaller bat. A different creature.

Justine's headlights flickered. Her engine struggled to stay alive.

The bat broke away from the Mustang and landed beside Penn. It changed into its more human form.

Isaac!

His rattlesnake fangs glistened in the moonlight, and he said, "I'm feeling a little better than I did before."

Penn hugged his brother and nearly cried.

And then he remembered Isaac was a vampire when the sixth-grader sniffed the air and licked his lips, looking hungrily at the bloody scrape on Penn's forearm.

Penn shoved Isaac away. "Don't even think about it."

"I don't want to. Really. But it's hard to resist." Isaac placed Edgar Allan Poe's quill into Penn's hand. "I went back home for this. You've got to end the story."

"Huh?"

"What you wrote . . . All these antagonists . . . What they've done, what they're capable of . . . I think it's because you used the quill."

"It's like magic or something, right?"

Isaac nodded. "Must be. All the violence, all the suspense . . . It's just going to keep going on and on and on . . . keep building . . . keep getting worse and worse . . . Because the story you started . . . the characters in it . . . They don't know where else to go . . . what else to do . . . how else to be . . . They're monsters. They're going to keep being monstrous until you stop them."

"Okay . . ."

"So, give the story an ending! A resolution! Use the quill, and stop all of this!"

Penn gestured to the sky. "But the paper's up there."

"I'll get it for you. Just think of something good to write. No more monsters. That includes me, okay? I don't want to be a vampire. Life's going to suck like this."

"I know. Sorry."

"Make me normal again, Penn."

"I will."

"I want to like sunshine. Not fear it."

"Got it."

"Drinking blood . . ." Isaac sighed. "That's going to be awful. I don't want that."

"I understand."

"Whatever you write, let me proofread it first. Make sure it doesn't get us into any more trouble, okay?"

"Yeah. All right."

After that, Isaac, a winged bullet, was off.

Then came a sequence of booming woofs. Hugo had finally earned himself entry into the middle school, and now he wanted in on the fun.

As large as he was, the Rottweiler seemed to move like a cheetah. He'd be on Penn in no time.

Beside the boy, Justine was dead quiet. Unmoving. So was Emmy inside the cab.

The hammer.

Penn needed it, and he needed it fast.

He crawled into Justine's cab through the open driver's side window. He pulled himself over shattered glass, around twisted bits of metal. He prayed the car wouldn't suddenly jumpstart back to life.

She didn't. But Emmy did.

Once Penn reached for her hammer, she grabbed him by the bloody forearm.

"Keep things as is!" she shouted in his face. "Don't change anything!"

"Let! Go!"

"Give me my autograph! Come on! For your number-one fan!"

He gave her an autograph, all right. He jabbed the pointed tip of the quill into her throat three times, until she finally released him to hold her neck shut.

Suddenly, Hugo was there, at the window, chomping at Penn's feet. Penn yelped, scooting as far back into the cab as he could. Emmy mewled some kind of frail objection as Penn pressed back against her.

Hugo climbed in after him, jamming his muscular body into the car. The dog snarled as he inched himself closer and closer. The beast's fetid breath roared hot against Penn's legs.

Penn moved the quill to his left hand and took Emmy's hammer in his right, prepared to use the weapon even though his arm throbbed with pain.

There wasn't enough space in the cramped cab for Penn to bring the weapon down on top of Hugo's encroaching snout. So the boy decided to sidearm his swing, like a baseball pitcher throwing a slider.

The hammer whacked against Hugo's upper jaw, breaking away some of the animal's teeth. Penn sidearmed the hammer again, again, again, shattering more of the monster's mouth.

Hugo upchucked a blend of acid and blood onto Penn's right hand and wrist. Penn dropped the hammer and wailed. He'd been scalded by hot sinkwater before, but this pain was infinitely worse. His skin bubbled and blistered.

With both feet, Penn kicked, kicked, kicked at Hugo's ruined mouth, finally driving the injured dog out of the vehicle. The Rottweiler, whimpering, scampered off into the darkness.

Penn dragged himself out of Justine's cab, tightly clutching the quill.

Above him, bats battled. Another dogfight was happening up there.

Penn couldn't see what was happening very clearly, but Isaac certainly wasn't giving up, even if the other vampire was twice his size.

The story broke free.

As it fell to the ground, it twisted and turned on the wind. With his eyes, Penn followed the paper's descent. He pocketed the quill and reached out for the tale with his left hand.

He caught it, looking at his handwriting in the moonlight. He shook his head, still not quite believing the power of his own words.

He carried the paper to the car. Using the side of the Mustang as a flat surface, Penn took the quill and began to finally write his ending.

Because he wasn't left-handed and his right hand was pretty much useless, it took a while for Penn to put something down on the page. He did his best to focus, even though he flirted for a moment with just giving up and tearing the story to shreds.

But, who knew what the consequences of that might actually be?

Would the nightmare just live on and on and on because it technically never got its end?

Would everything around him, including Isaac, tear to pieces along with the paper?

So, even though it was difficult, Penn wrote.

The bats continued their bout.

Penn wrote some more.

Ultimately, what he came up with was simple, but he thought it would get the job done just fine.

"*The boy's nightmare was suddenly over. Sunlight shined through a bedroom window. As it turned out, the crazy events of that night had all just been part of a really bad dream. It was time to go to school. What a relief!*"

Penn thought it was the perfect conclusion. But Isaac had said he wanted to review everything before it was deemed complete.

Penn shouted to the sky, "Isaac! I'm done! Isaac, get down here!"

But the bats' battle would not cease.

Then came a rumbling growl on Penn's left.

Hugo was back. Broken but angrier than ever. Bearing down on Penn like a runaway train.

Penn had no choice. He wrote six more letters on the paper.

"*T-H-E E-N-D*".

⊗   ⊗   ⊗

Penn opened his eyes to find his head on his desk. Drool had partially glued notebook paper to his cheek.

He bolted upright in his seat, glanced at the alarm clock, and scanned the room. He was alone.

Sunlight beamed through the bedroom window. It was almost time to leave for school.

"Oh, my God!" He pumped a fist. "No way!" His forearm wasn't sliced open. His hand wasn't disfigured by acid.

Wow! That had absolutely been the worst, most vivid nightmare of his entire life! Penn hoped to never see any of those monsters ever again.

He ripped a few movie posters away from his walls.

Down went *Eden's Plot*... *Hugo*... *Justine*... *Agony*... *Headless Horseman's Hollow*...

"Sorry, Grandpa."

Outside, a little dog yipped. Penn peered through his window, smiling when he saw Mr. Saint taking Pumpkin for a morning stroll.

Penn went back to the desk and read the story he'd fallen asleep on.

The ending was the same one he'd written inside his dream. Which was sort of strange, but whatever. At least he'd finished the assignment. Mr. Fairchild couldn't fail him now.

Except, the narrative still needed a title.

Penn took the paper with him next door, to his brother's room. The space was fairly dark. The curtains were drawn shut. A sliver of sun shined through a gap in the cloth.

"Isaac! Hey! I need your help, real quick!"

The smaller boy was in bed, still asleep, arms folded over *The Collected Works of Edgar Allan Poe*. The quill was back in place, sticking out of the book's spine.

Isaac must have put it there after Penn passed out at his desk.

Isaac whimpered. Cried out weakly, "No... Please... Stop... No..."

He was having a bad dream, too. What were the odds?

Penn shook Isaac's shoulder. "Hey, wake up."

Isaac still slept. Still quivered with fear.

Penn shook Isaac again. His brother would not wake.

"Isaac! Come on!"

Nope. Still trapped in slumber.

"Isaac."

He smacked Isaac across the cheeks, softly. Then, he did it harder.

The kid would. Not. Wake. Up.

Penn's brain then went back to the ending of his story. By the sliver of sunlight, he re-read what he had written. Once. Twice. Three times.

"Oh, no," he said. "No, no, no!"

Penn had been so eager to end the terror, so eager to write "*THE END*," that he hadn't bothered to check his work.

"*The boy's nightmare was suddenly over.*"

That's what he had written.

"*The boy's nightmare . . .*"

"*The boy's . . .*"

Not "*The* boys' *nightmare . . .*" Not both boys' terror coming to an end.

Just "*The* boy's . . ."

One boy.

Only one of them got a reprieve.

Penn's nightmare had met its conclusion.

Isaac's had not.

Isaac was still having a terrifying time. Because of Penn's mistake. Because of Penn's hastiness.

"ISAAC! WAKE UP, OKAY?! WAKE UP!"

Penn went to the window. He threw open the curtains. A torrent of sunlight spilled into the room, across Isaac's bed.

"COME ON! GET UP, ISAAC! GET UP!"

Isaac burst into flame.

The boy jumped to his feet, fully awake now, screaming in

agony. For mercy!

He dropped *The Collected Works of Edgar Allan Poe*, unharmed, to the floor.

Rattlesnake fangs began to char between his screeching lips.

"ISAAC! NO!"

He was still a vampire! Of course! Because his nightmare had never officially ended!

Penn yanked the curtains back into place, removing sunshine from the room.

Isaac continued to burn.

"Get in the shower!" Penn shouted. "We'll stop it in there!"

Isaac raced down the hallway, into the bathroom, where, thankfully, there weren't any windows. Penn was only a few steps behind him.

Isaac threw open the shower door, twisted the "COLD" knob all the way to the right, and howled beneath a steady stream of water.

The bathroom filled with smoke. Penn coughed, fanning the air with a towel. At least the blaze had died.

Somewhere nearby, a smoke alarm blared. From their room, Mom and Dad eventually asked what the heck was going on out there.

In terrible shape, Isaac trembled at the bottom of the shower. Much of his clothing had fused to his skin.

"The quill, Penn," Isaac grunted, flashing his fangs at his brother. "Get the quill ... I think you've ... you've got some ... some rewriting to do."

THE TELL-TALE ART

DON'T LOOK AT ME like that! Like you think I'm crazy. I can't stand that! I'm totally sane, all right?

The police—the doctors—they look at me the same way. And it makes the anger boil in my stomach. Makes it churn, makes it burn like a thousand suns. Until it rises up, up to my chest, filling my heart, hugging my soul tight.

If I had a knife, a fork, a spoon—anything!—I'd take the eyes right out of everyone's stupid skull. I'd bounce them off these walls like marbles. At least that would give me something to do. Something to make the time here pass me by. And I wouldn't have to be subjected to judgmental gazes any longer.

That would be amazing. Peaceful. Perfect.

Wait, wait! Please! Don't go! No one will listen to me. They say they'll listen, but they never really do. They only hear what they want to hear, only focus on the parts of the story that make me seem like a bad guy.

But I'm not a bad guy. I'm just misunderstood.

Give me a chance, will you? Time to explain myself, to tell my side of things.

I need someone in my corner. A confidant. A friend.

That could be you, right?

Right?

Great! Thank you! A million times, thank you!

Just stay right there. Sit. Relax. And try not to be like all the others. Have an open mind. Okay?

Okay?

Okay, fantastic!

Now, all of this took place over a decade ago, back when I was still a kid, so I'm not exactly sure when he first put the idea inside my head, but once it was in there, it latched on for dear life, and it was all I could think about. Other than all of the homework and the disgusting cafeteria food, I honestly liked Poe Middle School just fine.

But when I finally decided to torch the place down to the ground, there was no turning back.

He wouldn't let me change my mind.

Giggles the Clown. Otherwise known as Mr. Lacy.

You know about him. Everyone's heard that story. He was the Art teacher at Poe back in the sixties and seventies. Turns out he didn't make much money as an educator, so on the weekends he worked as a clown at kids' parties.

And sometimes he moonlit as a serial killer.

Yep. Ol' Giggles kept tabs on "special" children who caught his attention at those shindigs. He'd snatch them from their beds in the middle of the night, take them back to his house, and chop them up for supper.

Some say he went cannibal because of a nasty brain tumor. Others say he was just born bad. I say working fifteen years in a middle school pushed him over the edge. Since he couldn't fully unleash his frustrations on the punks in his classes, he raged against other young people who he deemed worthy of retribution.

The cops eventually found pieces of missing kids buried beneath Mr. Lacy's basement floor. The inedible parts, I guess.

Needless to say, Mr. Lacy's career as a teacher ended the day he was caught. I heard he stopped clowning around once he was in prison, too. They gave him the death penalty.

Mr. Lacy's been dead for about twenty years now.

And, ever since, he's been haunting the school where he once taught.

Not many people know this, but, before he was jailed, Mr. Lacy painted a portrait of himself as Giggles. He displayed it in his classroom. After that, it was moved into the custodian's closet located at the far end of the Science wing's second floor. The grinning clown hung there for years, behind metal shelves lined with cleaning supplies.

In the painting, Mr. Lacy smiled wide behind ghostly white make-up. His eyes were shadowed in blue and green. He wore a rainbow afro wig and a matching puffy, striped jumpsuit. He also wore a bulbous Rudolph the Reindeer-looking nose. He held a cluster of red balloons with one gloved hand and waved at the viewer with the other.

The crimson in the artwork didn't come just from paint, by the way. No, Mr. Lacy mixed in some of his own blood. This eerie creative choice was one the teacher ultimately came to regret. For, unbeknownst to him at the time, his blood tied him to that piece of art. Meaning, his spirit could not move past this earthly plane and on to the Other Side. Mr. Lacy's phantom was doomed to wander the grounds of Poe Middle School.

His ghost first appeared to me a few days after I was caught tagging on desks and textbooks in my Algebra class. A girl I crushed on at the time had dared me to do it. I thought doing something "bad" would make me look cool or dangerous. I wasn't a very smart kid or all that experienced at being "bad," so I didn't know I wasn't supposed to use my actual name when vandalizing school property.

Oops. Man, I was dumb.

Instead of allowing me to be suspended like any other delinquent, my parents agreed to have me assist with campus cleanup after school for a week. I was told to meet Mr. Davidson, the kindly old custodian, at the closet located at the far end of the

Science wing's second floor.

That's how I first came across the clown's creepy painting.

Mr. Davidson must've been a lonely guy, because he talked to me a whole lot during that week I spent as his "sweeping sidekick". Among other things, the man explained that it was his job to keep the school looking nice, but it was also his responsibility to keep students and staff safe from harm. He told me the history of Mr. Lacy's portrait and the fact that it was his duty to keep it hidden from view. The task had been passed on to him from the previous custodian.

Mr. Davidson said that, in the past, scary stuff had happened to anyone who tried to remove the artwork from the school. In other words, the painting was cursed. That news sent icy spiders crawling up and down my spine.

Then I began to see the clown standing in the hallways and staring at me from the corners of my classrooms. No one else could see him, not even Mr. Davidson. People thought I was a lunatic whenever I told them he was near. I guess that once I saw Mr. Lacy's masterpiece, I was marked by his spirit. Not just any student got to see the work of art, after all. I was a rare case. I was "special".

People looked at me like I was "special," all right. So I eventually stopped mentioning the clown. I pretended that he wasn't there.

But he was: every day at school. Every class. Every period. Holding those red balloons. Waving at me, smiling. Never speaking, never making a single sound—at least, not at first.

Obviously, I couldn't concentrate on my schoolwork. I couldn't eat, I couldn't sleep. Even when I was at home, away from the clown, I thought I could feel him close by, just out of sight. My grades dropped immediately.

I tried skipping school, tried convincing my parents that I should go somewhere else. But they thought I was just being a difficult adolescent. That it was merely some kind of a phase.

Oh, how I wish it had just been a brief chapter in my life

story! Something that would eventually pass.

But it wasn't. It was constant torment. Everlasting agony.

And, so, I can't remember exactly when or where, Mr. Lacy, the sadistic clown, my walking nightmare, at long last whispered into my ear that he wanted me to do something for him. He giggled as he told me his dark desire.

He wanted me to destroy Poe Middle School, once and for all. To set him free. He promised it would set me free, as well.

My memory's fuzzy in spots, but I do, indeed, think he called me "special". He told me that not just any idiot could do what he needed done.

Again, I did my best to ignore the monster. But he was relentless. He refused to be silent. He persisted, day in and day out. He cackled and grinned at my misery, at my tears.

Finally, *finally*, months after I had scared the last of my friends away, I nodded in agreement. I squeaked weakly to the horrible beast that yes, *yes*, I would do what he wanted.

The school would burn. It would burn, burn, *burn*!

But my declaration did not quiet the clown. No, it only fueled his fire. Now he kept asking me when, *when* would I do the deed? How long would he have to wait? It needed to be done soon, soon, *soon*!

Now, I knew that what I was planning was wrong, that it was awful, and that it could get me into a heap of trouble. But that was only if I was caught.

I had to be clever about my crime. Very clever.

It wasn't long before I began to enjoy the process of planning the dastardly deed. I enjoyed using my brain for a purpose other than fearing the clown. I filled a notebook with sketches and ideas. I worked in it every time a teacher turned away from me, every free moment I had at home.

Torturous Mr. Lacy could see how hard I focused on his task. How much I needed to concentrate. Still, he hovered over me, reminding me often that I needed to leave his painting unscathed.

Eventually, Giggles stopped giggling and gave me some room

to breathe.

But that terrible smile never left his face.

The scheme took a few weeks to finalize. It went through many forms and variations. In the end, it wound up being rather uncomplicated. The genius was in its simplicity.

My first step was to learn how to pick a lock. It took some time, but I watched tutorial videos online. Before too long, I was an expert with my mother's hairpins.

The next step was to siphon gasoline from my father's car into some empty water bottles. I was able to accomplish this at night, after watching more videos, while my parents were lost in dreamland. I used plastic tubing and a small pump that I had purchased at a hardware store. The clerk had seemed suspicious that I would use my allowance money on such items, but I assured her that I was only buying supplies for a Science Fair project.

Then, I made sure to delete my Internet history. I triple-checked that my solid black hoodie sweatshirt was out of the laundry. That my ski mask and snow gloves were out of storage. That my tennis shoes were well broken in.

Finally, late on a Friday, I walked right out the front door. My parents were snoozing after a long night of ignoring me and drinking red wine. Backpack tightly secured, I jogged the few blocks to the middle school.

Once outside the chain-linked fence that surrounded Poe, I unzipped my bag. I removed my ski mask and snow gloves and slipped them on. I pulled the black hood of my sweatshirt over my head, further obscuring my identity.

I hopped the fence and ran along the side of the school, heading for the doors that led into the Science wing. From a distance, I could see that they were chained shut, held together by a single lock. Once I reached the closed entrance, I pulled my tools from the backpack.

I did not hesitate. I shoved a couple of hairpins into the lock and began to work. I had done this a thousand times in my head and a few dozen times on my bedroom doorknob.

Within minutes, the lock unlatched. No one could see the smile under my mask. I unchained the doors and pulled them open.

I stepped onto the first floor of the Science wing and pulled the doors shut behind me. In the dark hallway, I could make out a small security camera in the ceiling. It pointed my way.

Every floor in the school had cameras like these. I didn't know if any of them worked. But, in case they did, I had worn my disguise for this very thing.

I raced upstairs to the second floor and stopped when I saw a figure lingering in the shadows. Giggles the Clown. I had told him tonight was the night.

He walked toward me as I jimmied the lock on the custodian's closet, reaching my side just as I turned the bolt and threw the door open. Mr. Lacy giggled and clapped his hands.

I flipped a light switch, went to the shelves, and pulled down every bottle and aerosol can I could find.

Mr. Davidson really needed to do a better job of staying in compliance with school safety standards. Any pyromaniac would have had a field day with the arsenal he kept in that closet.

I unscrewed and kicked over anything that contained flammable liquid. A stinking puddle formed in the middle of the tiny room. I tossed aerosol cans into the putrid pond, where they teetered like capsizing boats.

I then took Mr. Lacy's portrait down from the wall and turned back to the doorway. I was careful not to step in the puddle or to breathe too deeply. The fumes could have knocked me out.

I rested the cursed picture, unharmed, against the open doorframe.

I removed bottles of gasoline from my backpack. I poured smelly trails from the closet to the doors of the two nearest classes. I knew Mr. Avalos and Ms. Rogers kept potentially hazardous chemicals in their rooms for experimental purposes.

The chemicals were about to reach their full potential, that was for sure.

A short while later, I had those classroom doors wide open. I poured the remainder of the gasoline over wooden desks and chairs and over vulnerable electrical equipment. I placed the empty bottles inside my backpack.

The chain reaction fire that would rage in this section of the school would spread like a plague, devouring everything in its path. No one—*nothing*!—would be able to quell its hunger.

That was the vision. The goal. The dream.

When I exited Ms. Rogers's room, Giggles the Clown still stood outside the custodian's closet. He gave me a thumbs-up and grinned.

I nodded and gave him a thumbs-up, too.

He thought I was taking his portrait home with me.

But he had no idea what I had planned next.

Back at the closet, I took Mr. Lacy's prized painting from where it leaned against the doorway and carefully placed it into the chemical puddle, where it gently splashed. I jumped back a little. I wanted none of the flammable liquid to touch my clothing, in case the fire decided it wanted a piece of me.

I exited the closet, stepping over the winding river of gasoline that snaked down the hallway. The clown was happy no more. He gestured toward his beloved artwork, now submerged helplessly beneath the surface of the unfriendly lake.

I shrugged and told him we were through. He was absolutely going down in flames. My hope was that he would feel every bit of the pain he had inflicted upon me. He would be free, all right. But not before he suffered terribly by my hands.

From my backpack, I removed a small book of matches that my father had brought home from a seedy bar. The clown tried to wave me off. He had second thoughts now that he knew he was going to burn fast and furious along with the school.

I struck a match. A puny flame danced before my eyes. It grew once I held it against the end of the matchbook, setting the entire thing ablaze.

I showed it to Mr. Lacy, taunted him with it. He shook a finger at me and scolded me fiercely.

I laughed at him and tossed the burning matchbook into the closet. It landed in the puddle with a roar.

Immediately, orange fire blasted upward and outward. Intense heat pressed me closer to the wall across from the closet. For the first few moments, I did not take my eyes off the blaze.

Beside me, the clown screamed. He fell to his knees, clawing at himself in vain as paint slowly melted down his cheeks like candlewax. The balloons in his grasp popped one by one by one by one.

As his artwork was incinerated, his evil soul agonized.

The conflagration sped from the closet, past us, along the gasoline path, into the classrooms I had doused with accelerant. Soon, enormous flames engulfed the classroom doors.

I turned to run away from the blaze.

Suddenly, something exploded in the closet behind me. I was thrown hard against the wall, and I slid to the floor, dazed and aching. Fireballs rained down upon me, quickly eating through my hood and ski mask, searing my scalp. No longer thinking about concealing my identity, I tore the sweatshirt and mask free. I stomped the fire out of the clothing.

The hallway was thick with smoke now. I choked and coughed, inhaling ash and fumes.

Mr. Lacy tried pitifully to crawl away from the destruction. His flesh was bubbling and charred black, eaten away in some spots to reveal bone under the skin. His spirit was done.

Well-done.

He would soon be free. But not from his pain.

I stuffed my scorched clothes into my backpack. My work here was finished.

I rocketed downstairs and sped out through the doors on the ground floor. In the distance, sirens approached.

Somehow, I managed to run even faster. I was a cheetah on steroids, back over the fence and away from the sweltering carnage in no time flat. On my way home, I never came across a single fire truck or police car.

I had gotten away with it! The perfect crime!

My parents didn't awaken when I sneaked past their closed bedroom door, not even when I hacked up some ash still stuck in my throat.

Back in my room, I threw down the backpack and peeled off my gloves and shoes. I lay on my bed and beamed, convinced that I wouldn't close my eyes for hours, that I would ride my adrenaline high into a glorious night sky.

Images of the crispy clown flooded my mind. Never would I hear his laugh again. If I ever needed a smile, I would only have to think of his pathetic cries!

I chuckled to myself. And coughed some more.

Then I heard it.

Over there, in the corner, behind my open closet door.

A familiar giggle.

No! No, no, *no*!

The sneering clown showed himself, dragging his mangled body across the carpet with singed fingers. His face was unrecognizable beneath blistering wounds. Most of his wig was gone or burned black. His red ball nose now looked like a ruined campfire marshmallow. But it was him, all right, giggling like a fool.

Mr. Lacy had followed me home.

But how? How, how, *how*?

I finally noticed an acrid stench. The smell of smoke.

It was me. I was covered in soot. Likely, bits of the destroyed painting had floated through the air and stuck to me, keeping the clown alive, bringing him home after all.

I removed the blanket from my bed and picked up my backpack and tennis shoes. I raced to the garage.

Once there, I unzipped the backpack and took out the plastic bottles, throwing them aside. They bounced loudly across the concrete floor. I pulled out the ski mask and sweatshirt. I tore off what I wore and crammed every bit of clothing into the washing machine. The blanket, backpack, and shoes went in, too. Next, I poured in a flood of detergent and started the wash cycle.

I then went to the bathroom, locked the door, and showered. I shampooed the smoky stink right out of my hair, scrubbed the grime and ash off my skin.

The clown had to disappear now. He just had to!

A fist pounded against the door. Mr. Lacy? Still?

I yelled, "Go away!" but it wasn't him.

It was my mother. Apparently, my shoes thundering around inside the washing machine had woken her.

I had to explain to her why I was showering so late, and why I was cleaning my shoes, backpack, ski mask, and gloves in the middle of the night. Of course, I lied and said that I needed a clean costume for a video I had to make for English class. She didn't look like she believed me, but she told me to hang up the shoes and backpack after the wash so they wouldn't break the dryer. Then, she returned to bed.

Back in my room, I slipped into some pajamas. The clown crept out from under the bed, giggling. I shrieked.

My mother ran in to see what was wrong. I pointed to the cackling spirit, but she saw nothing. No matter how much I insisted. No matter how loudly Mr. Lacy laughed.

My mother's eyes were sad. I could tell that she was disappointed that I was talking about the ghost again. She must've thought that I'd grown out of it.

To get her to leave, I told her I was only joking. She didn't think it was funny. Neither did I.

I didn't sleep that night. The clown wouldn't allow it. He called me a failure. He said he would never leave me now. That he was a part of me.

In a way, he was.

I had inhaled bits of his flaming painting. Swallowed the microscopic pieces. They now rested, wedged, in my lungs, absorbed by my body tissue.

As long as I breathed, the clown would be there nearby. He

was officially no longer tied to the school.

He was attached to me.

For days, the papers and television news reported on the fire at Poe Middle. Ninety percent of the school had burned down before firefighters finally killed the blaze. The place had to be completely rebuilt.

Because the security cameras went down with the school, Mr. Davidson was charged with the crime. As luck would have it, the custodian had been in a recent argument with the principal over his work hours and pay. Poor Mr. Davidson, the perfect patsy.

It didn't sit well in my stomach that an innocent man would pay for my misdeeds.

Despite Mr. Davidson's arrest, my mother looked at me like she suspected I might have had a part in the fiery incident. My actions that night still mystified her.

Then Mr. Lacy started telling me that I had to kill her. He claimed that my own mother might go to the police with her suspicions.

He said I had to make it look like an accident. Or that I could even frame my father for the homicide.

I begged him to stop, to shut up, but he never did. He just giggled and told me how to get away with murder. He was an expert on the subject, after all.

He told me how things would be better with them gone. I would have the freedom every kid desired.

All I wanted was freedom from him. But it was impossible. As long as I lived, he had life.

My thoughts grew darker by the day. But I didn't want to hurt myself. Did I?

The weight of it all was too much to bear. Like a herd of elephants stacked on top of a Jenga tower.

It wasn't long before I broke down to my parents and told them everything. How Mr. Lacy lamented that I was a fool, fool, *fool*! How he hated my decision!

Which was precisely why I did it.

It was my way of taking back control. I wouldn't allow the clown to steer the course of my destiny, to doom me once more. No way. Not again. The power was back in my hands.

My saddened parents took me to the police station, where I confessed that I had razed the school. I convinced them to let Mr. Davidson go, although the detectives didn't buy what I said about Mr. Lacy's phantom. All they had to do was look down at their feet and see that he was in the room, crawling around us like a lizard, but the stupid officers never gave my story a real chance.

They only looked at me like I was crazy.

The doctors here at the hospital don't believe the ghost haunts me, either. They never have. Even though I've been telling them for ten years now that he's here with me!

Every day I tell them and every day Mr. Lacy continues to try to convince me to escape. To maim. To kill.

I see it in your eyes. You think I'm making it up too, right? Just like all the others. You think I'm a liar and a freak.

Well, you don't have to take my word for it. Turn around. Go ahead. Do it. There he is, right there, behind you.

The clown. Don't you hear him giggling?

Don't you hear his hideous laugh?

Don't you?

LOCKER A256

IT TOOK THIRTEEN MONTHS to rebuild Poe Middle School. A massive fire had devastated the campus, reducing much of it to rubble.

In one hallway, however, a few rows of lockers remained unscathed. Even as everything collapsed and burned around them, the lockers seemingly took no damage.

It was almost like the roaring flames had deliberately danced around them. As if the inferno had allowed the lockers to linger.

During reconstruction, the lockers were painted to look brand-new. But they were the same exact lockers from before, holding the same exact secrets behind their doors.

The night before Poe was to reopen to hundreds of students, the lockers reopened to the world. Shadowy figures, slithery monstrosities, and stealthy spirits slunk off into various corners of the school, ready to reclaim the institution as their own.

It was time again for them to influence those who ventured through their domain.

Only one locker stayed shut.

A single cell held its prisoner secure.

A256.

From inside, fists pounded against metal. A teenage boy begged for release.

Something pulled him back into gloom. The boy's screams echoed in the hall.

Soon, they were gone and replaced by the purrs of a bored, old cat.

Locker A256 would perhaps open again.

But only if its guardian deemed an individual worthy of the darkness within.

ACKNOWLEDGMENTS

EVER SINCE I WAS a boy hooked on nightmarish narratives of ghosts and monsters (Thank you, Edgar Allan Poe and other makers of the macabre!), I have dreamt of publishing my own spooky collection of short stories. I worked on these thirteen tales for many, many years, fine-tuning them into what you see before you today. There are a number of people who have assisted me on my creative writing journey, individuals who have believed in my work and have encouraged me to write more and write often. I am thankful to have had each of them in my corner.

For a long while, I was uncertain that these stories would ever find a home or an audience. Thanks go to Jonathan W. Thurston Howl for taking a chance on me, for embracing my darkness, for pushing me to make these stories bigger and better, and for even daring to set foot inside the twisted halls of Edgar Allan Poe Middle School in the first place.

Mom and Dad, thank you for always allowing me to pursue my writing dreams. I know that you haven't always understood my love of horror, but you never once told me to stop imagining monsters or to stop imagining that I would someday have success as an author. I love you.

I am grateful for the Fictioneers: Jessica, Alan, Sergio, and Christine. I could not do what I do without the support of other writers. You four have helped me more than you know. You always find nice things to say about my work, even when bad things are happening on the page. I am thankful for your honest critiques, our monthly get-togethers, and for your friendship. I champion your writing, as well, and I look forward to seeing all of your books on my shelf one day.

Thank you, Pat Dobie, for reading and editing an earlier draft of this collection. Your kind words and suggestions helped me to polish this manuscript into something worth reading.

To the fine folks at Chicago's Small Fish Radio Theatre and Thespinarium, I give thanks for your continued interest in my fiction, and for producing a number of my pieces in your annual Halloween shows. Your dramatization of "Loud Mouths" is one of my favorites.

I thank the editors at Gypsum Sound Tales for including "It's a Zoo in There" in their magazine, *Colp: A Little Bit of Nonsense*. "Zoo" is a weird, wild story, and I'm grateful that you were the first to share my little bit of nonsense with the world.

To my students of past, present, and future, thank you for making every day an adventure. Middle schoolers are an interesting lot. You're never boring, and this book would not have been possible without having you in my classroom. Over the years, you've sparked much of my creativity. Thank you for the memories. (Even the scary ones.) It has taken time for me to reach this personal milestone, and I hope that you never give up your own dreams. With hard work, dedication, and resiliency, you can also accomplish what is important to you.

And to You, the Reader: I appreciate the time you have spent at Poe Middle School. I hope you were satisfied with your stay. I built the place just for you.

A final thank you goes to The Emaciated Man. You have gifted me countless riches and a life of purpose, Master. As an offering, I have brought these unsuspecting souls into your world.

May you find your way to these bloodthirsty readers of the macabre and deem them worthy of consumption.

ABOUT THE AUTHOR

EVAN BAUGHFMAN WORKS IN a very scary place: a middle school! (He's a totally-not-evil teacher.) He lives in California with his wife, Ashley, his children, Mason and Story, and their probably-not-evil-at-all black cat, Friday. Evan has been reading and writing for fun since childhood. After disturbing his mom with a tale about killer opossums, Evan knew that he wanted to write a book of his own someday. Evan was so serious about becoming an author that he earned a Bachelor's degree in Creative Writing from University of Redlands.

Evan writes all genres, but horror is where he is most comfortable. His short fiction has also appeared in publications from Black Hare Press, Blood Song Books, Soteira Press, Emerald Bay Books, and Grinning Skull Press.

Much of Evan's writing success has been as a playwright. He's had many different plays produced across the globe. Heuer Publishing has published Evan's script, "A Taste of Amontillado" (an adaptation of Edgar Allan Poe's "The Cask of Amontillado"), in addition to a couple of his other scripts. Evan's work can also be found at YouthPLAYS, Drama Notebook, and New Play Exchange.

Furthermore, Evan has adapted a number of his Terrifying Tales into short film screenplays, of which "The Emaciated Man", "The Tell-Tale Art," and "A Perfect Circle" have all won awards in various film festival competitions.

More information about Evan's writing can be found at his website, *www.evanbaughfman.com*

Made in the USA
Las Vegas, NV
03 November 2020

10539628R00089